# It's Wendy

## on the

## Outside

Marilyn Turner

# Dedication

This book is dedicated to...

All High school teens who are struggling to find their identity and purpose. And to all the parents who are helping them navigate through the various teenage road blocks  of this age. Hang in there, your light will come.

For He knows the plan He has for you.
Jeremiah 29:11

# Acknowledgments

With special thanks to:

**The cast of *It's Wendy On The Outside* stage play:**
Thank you all for your enthusiasm and professionalism. I'm looking forward to presenting this story on stage.

**For sure, to my NHIM Worship Center church family:**
You are so dope, all of you.

**My family:**
Thank you for your supportive love.

**My loving and supportive husband, Apostle Charles Turner III:**
Thank you for your love and for always holding me accountable to my assignments. I love you to life!

**Lastly, and most importantly, because I can do nothing without Him:**
My Lord and Savior. Thank you, Jesus, for giving me this story and the gift of storytelling.

# Table of Contents

# Foreword

Marilyn Turner has did it again, and as always, she did not disappoint! In this book, she has created a very fascinating character by the name of Wendy. Wendy is not your typical teenager; she's a leader who doesn't want to lead. She's a young woman who doesn't seem to have boys on her mind. What I find interesting about the Wendy character is her laid-back approach to life, and what I find interesting about this story is the series of events that had to take place in order to catapult Wendy into the very role she had been running from, and that is a leadership role.

Additionally, I love how Marilyn weaves so many characters together into one story, ensuring that each character has his or her own unique personality. In truth, you will find that some of the characters may remind you of some of the people you know.

This book is nothing short of masterful or, better yet, genius. There are so many life-lessons, laughs and unforgettable moments in this book. You will find it hard to put down! All the same, reading It's Wendy on the Outside is like watching a really good movie, so I suggest that you grab yourself a few snacks, put on your favorite pajamas and enjoy the masterpiece that you're about to read!

Tiffany Buckner
Anointed Fire

# Chapter One

# A Day in the Life of Wendy

The light of a new day is beginning to peep through the bay windows of the living room where Wendy is sleeping. The darkness of the previous night fades away as the morning approaches, causing the room to appear as if it's hosting a hazy fog. Wendy is in a deep sleep, but her body is positioned oddly across a red velvet love seat. Though pretty and chic, the love seat doesn't look like it was designed to get a good night's sleep on.

Her breathing is steady until she seems to stop breathing for a moment. Without warning, she releases a quick snort through her nose, followed by a choking cough. This causes her to roll right out of her awkward sleeping position and onto the hardwood floor. She lands partly under the coffee table just missing the plush rug that would have helped soften the fall. She lands on the floor in an awkward position. The loud thud her body makes on impact awakens her.

She makes an inaudible sound, and for the next few moments, she lays as still as the quietness in the house. Finally, she lifts a hand and begins to grope around the edge of the coffee table in search for her phone. She locates it, swings it to her face and, like clockwork, swipes the screen with her thumb in order to read the alarm. It's 5:58 am, just two minutes before her alarm is set to go off.

For a moment, Wendy is tempted to reset it, giving herself another half hour before she begins her day. Instead, she thinks about the consequences of being the last person in a long line for the bathroom. In the past and under much different circumstances, Wendy didn't have to rise so early in the morning in order to get herself together and off to school everyday. But those times are gone and, more than likely, they are gone forever.

It's a full house since Aunt Gurley, Wendy's maternal aunt and her nine and ten-year-old boys, Eric and Frankie, moved in. The arrangement was made on the promise that "it would just be for a month or, at the most, two months." That was just until Gurley could find a new job and get back on her feet. At the time, it made better sense for Wendy to volunteer her bedroom to the small family, rather than have them take up residence in the living room. Two months came and went without any change. Several months later, Wendy was almost regretting her generosity.

Their presence wouldn't be so suffocating if Pop-Pop, Wendy's senile grandfather, hadn't moved into the spare room just a few months before them. In the beginning, it was pretty cool to have some company in the modest home that Wendy and her mother, Martha Lee Brown, had lived in since Wendy began first grade. It was like one big happy family. The boys' laughter and mischievous daily pranks make Wendy feel as if she's a legitimate big sister to siblings she's never had. And seeing her mother enjoying her sister's company from day-to-day has been an added bonus.

Dementia is not a glorious condition, but there sure are some funny moments, especially from the perspective of a teenager and a couple of preteen boys. And besides, Pop-Pop is in the early stages of Dementia, and in his more lucid moments, Wendy can count on his daily affirmations and famous quotes like clockwork to help get her through the tough moments.

All in all, Wendy hasn't grown weary enough to make complaints about the overcrowded house. She's okay with entertaining the boys, answering their gazillion questions about life, and helping them with their homework. Admittedly, sleeping on the couch, waking up on the floor, and racing to be the first in line for the bathroom every morning has become a bit of a headache, but she's beginning to accept that this way of life may just be their new normal. That is, at least until she graduates this Spring and moves away for college.

Wendy places her cell phone back on the table and begins the arduous process of getting to her feet. Finally standing, she picks up her bundle of clothes for the day and makes a beeline down the hallway because she knows time is of the essence and every moment counts. She lets out a relieved sigh as she presses her way past the bathroom door. Just as she is hanging her clothes on the hook on the back of the door, her cell phone alarm goes off threatening to wake up the entire house. She makes a mad dash back to the living room to shut off her alarm, before turning towards the hallway just in time to get a glimpse of the bare foot of a little person disappearing into the bathroom. She plops on the couch in despair as the door slams shut.

Moments later, Eric, the younger of the two boys, joins Wendy in the living room. He has his sneakers in his hands. As he sits next to Wendy on the couch, he shoves one of the shoes in her hands. "I can't get the knot out of this shoelace. Will you get it out like you did before?" he asks. Wendy responds with patience and a little playful sarcasm in her voice, "You mean, like I do every morning! What do you do to these shoes?" She begins to struggle with the knot. "Good lord, Eric! I keep telling you that you have to slow down when you take your shoes off!"

She continues to scold him as she rises to go to the kitchen. She was looking for a utensil to help her with the knot. "Looks as if one end of this lace was tied to a pole and the other to a tow truck!" She gets lost in the moment as she tries to untie the knot. After a minute, she hears the bathroom door open, and before she can move, Eric darts to his feet shouting, "It's about time, Frankie! I am about to pee my pants. What took you so long?!" Eric disappears behind the bathroom door before slamming it. Wendy sighs, "Ah, the story of my life! Got taken by a nine-year old yet again!"

She continues to wrestle with the knot as Frankie, fully dressed in khaki pants and a wrinkled white shirt, sits at the kitchen table and begins to put on his sneakers. He speaks to his cousin in a playful tone, "Oh, I see Eric got you again with the shoe trick. You know he's not even going to wear those shoes today, right?!" Wendy responds, "What do you mean? He's going to wear these shoes! What other shoes does he have but these?"

"Take off that shirt so I can press some of those wrinkles out," Wendy says, extending her right hand in Frankie's direction. Frankie stands up and begins to unbutton his shirt. He then takes it off and tosses it onto the kitchen table. He sits down and continues to tie the lace of one of his shoes. With a more serious tone, he says, "Hey, what would you do if you had a friend who likes the same girl that one of your other friends is dating?!!" Wendy finally gets the knot out of the shoelace and has a moment of celebration. "Yes! Whew! That knot was a firecracker, but it didn't win!"

She walks to the living room to reunite the sneaker with its mate. As she puts it down, she turns her attention back to Frankie's question. She then grabs the iron and the table top ironing board out of the broom closet and begins to set them up on the kitchen table. "Frankie, first of all, how old are you? Ten?! Ten, bro... what are you guys doing talking about you're 'dating'? When I was your age, I wasn't thinking about no boys..." Frankie cuts her off to say, "But, you're still not thinking about no boys... so..." After a brief moment of silence, Wendy begins to stumble over her words, "So... so, so, ... what?!! I... have better things to do..." She grabs his shirt and begins to tackle the wrinkles with the steam from the iron.

Frankie interjects, "Like what?!" Wendy finishes her sentence, "...than to chase after little boys..." Frankie interjects again, "But you're a teenager. Don't teenagers date other teenagers, and not little boys?" Wendy is exasperated. "You know what? It's too early in the morning to be talking about the dating game. Just tell your friend that it's better to focus on getting good grades rather than getting lost in some girl's pretty brown eyes. He needs to prepare himself for college; he can date when he graduates college with a degree and a job. Besides, he's too young to start making plans to take care of a girl because that eventually begets a family... Does he have a job? He needs to be dating Jesus! Oh yeah, and tell him to practice good hygiene habits too."

Frankie is so perplexed at his cousin's rambling that he responds by throwing both hands up in the air.

"Huh?!?!" he shouts just as the bathroom door opens. Eric darts out of the bathroom with a towel wrapped around his little body and makes his way back to the bedroom. Wendy then presents her little cousin with a freshly ironed shirt before attempting to make her way to the bathroom. Without warning, Pop-Pop staggers into view, and then disappears behind the bathroom doors. Wendy lets out a spontaneous silent sigh, accompanied by a few air punches and kicks.

Giggling at Wendy's reaction, Frankie snatches his shirt from her hand as he follows his little brother to the bedroom singing in his best James Brown voice, "It's a man's world." Wendy raises her once whispered voice to her little cousin, "What do you even know about that song, bro?! You're ten... tennnnn!!" Left alone in the kitchen, Wendy begins to talk out loud to herself, "Pop-Pop beat me to the bathroom... just what I didn't want to happen." She slaps her forehead with the palm of her hand as she whines, "Oh, why doesn't he ever remember that there is a bathroom in his bedroom?!" She throws her hands in the air and begins the task of putting the iron and the ironing board away.

A minute later, Gurley strolls into the kitchen dressed in a beautiful designer bathrobe. Her hair is pulled up into a bun, covered with a matching scarf tied into a perfect bow. She was also wearing slippers that matched her scarf. As perfect as her wardrobe appears to be at first glance, Wendy notices that something is off-kilter about her aunt's demeanor as Gurley saunters toward her.

Gurley is the younger version of her sister, Martha Lee (Wendy's mom), but only in outward appearances. They have the same flawless, chocolate brown skin, the same attractive facial features highlighting their almond-shaped caramel-colored eyes, beautiful full lips that reveal their perfect white teeth whenever they smile, and the same full figure. It would be difficult telling them apart if it weren't for the five inches in height Martha Lee has over her little sister. But height and age are not their only differences.

It's an oddity that they look so much alike, seeing they don't share the same father. Pop-Pop, whose name is Henry Brown, is Martha Lee's father, but not Gurley's. Before his health began to decline, he was a self-made grocer and one of the first successful small business owners in his community, where he was much loved and hailed as a hero. Martha Lee most definitely inherited her entrepreneurial spirit, sense of responsibility, and passion for people from Pop-Pop. On the other hand, Gurley is exactly the opposite of her big sister. A "me, myself, and I" type of person, she can be irresponsible and negligent when it comes to managing her life. One of the more pleasant qualities about her is her good-humor, but even that is in a dark kind of way.

Now that Gurley is standing a few feet away, Wendy can see what's off-kilter with her auntie. First, the saunter in her walk is actually a hung over stagger. Secondly, she has on a full face of makeup, which includes oversized mink eyelashes, electric blue eyeshadow, and bright red lipstick. It's obvious that the makeup is from the previous night since the falsies are playing peek-a-boo on her eyelids, lifting up and down and hanging on by a thread with every blink of Gurley's eyes. The electric blue eye shadow appears to be perfectly preserved while the lipstick is more like cheek stick. Lastly, she reeks of stale cigarette smoke and booze.

"Morning, Wendy", Gurley says, torturing Wendy with her morning 'club' breath. As she begins to stagger to the refrigerator, she continues, "It's too early this morning and I'm not feeling this. I'm wondering if you could make sure the boys have something to eat and they get off to school on time?!!" By this time, Gurley's hands are on the milk carton. She quickly unscrews the cap and turns the full carton up to her lips and begins to drink as if there is no end to her thirst. Wendy is shocked and speechless as she watches her auntie quench her thirst, return the top on the carton, and carefully place the milk almost exactly how she found it in the refrigerator.

Afterwards, she begins to walk off, but stops mid-stride to say, "Thanks. Oh, and I didn't get a chance to pack their lunch. Can you give them each a few dollars to buy their lunches today? I'll pay you back..." She makes her way back to the bedroom, leaving Wendy without audience as she responds. "Sure, you will, Auntie. I guess I will assume your responsibilities..." She suddenly flashes back to her first sight of her aunt's eyelashes, and she doesn't know whether to laugh or to be mad.

Just then, the bathroom door opens and Wendy makes a mad dash towards the bathroom. As she approaches the door, Pop-Pop steps out. He begins to give an apology of some sort. "I would use the bathroom in my bedroom, but if I do, I wouldn't be able to stay in the room afterwards." He then moves away from the doorway, and as he does, a gushing wind of 'morning doo' overwhelms her every sense. She whines under her breath, "I just can't right now!" As he staggers down the hall and just before he disappears inside his bedroom, he says in an incoherent voice, "Believe you can and you're halfway there. Theodore Roosevelt said that." Wendy takes a moment to recover and then takes a deep breath before walking into the bathroom and shutting the door.

Some time later, Wendy emerges from the bathroom fully dressed and sporting a full face of makeup and her signature oversized eyelashes, which actually add to her unique style in a tasteful kind of teenaged way. She's chosen to sweep her extra-long, blue-streaked box braided hair into an 'up do' style today; this is one of her go-to styles. As she approaches the living room where the boys are texting on their phones and making small talk with one another, she begins to complain about the condition of her school uniform. "Eric, I know it was you! What happened to the bottoms of my pant's legs?!!" Eric responds, "I don't know; they were just hanging on the hook and..." Laughing, Frankie cuts his brother off and says to Wendy, "What did happen? It looks like you went wading in the water." Wendy snaps back at him,

"Yeah, you got jokes this morning! How about you go lunchless today?!!"

He quickly changes his tone to a sober one as he responds, "Oh, Mom didn't make us lunch again?!!" There's a moment of silence before he speaks again, "Well, you know, your pants don't look so bad, cousin. They'll probably dry before you even arrive at school; it's cool." Wendy responds, "Oh, aren't you the sweet one?" She grabs some money out of her purse and distributes it between the two boys. "You know you're covered. I just hope the lunch food is good today." She chuckles as she grabs a piece of fruit for each of them from the fridge and tosses one to each. She then goes for the carton of milk, but quickly turns her direction to the orange juice instead, and pours a glass of it for herself.

Meanwhile, Eric decides to try his new prank toy out on Wendy. He pulls a string out of his pocket with what appears to be a toy mouse attached to it. As Wendy begins to drink her juice, he throws the toy mouse on the floor in front of her. He yells, "Oh, what's that?!! A mouse!" Wendy lets out a yelp and leaps higher than she ever thought she could, spilling the remainder of the orange juice onto the front of her white blouse. When the boys begin to laugh and she

13

realizes that the mouse was a prank, she quickly grabs a kitchen cloth, hoping to wipe away the orange juice before it sinks into the fabric. It was too late; her wiping only made the stain worse.

Frustrated, she begins to scold her cousins, "You guys... Not funny! Look what you made me do? Gosh!" Looking at her watch, she continues, "I don't have time to change! Does it look that bad?!!" As she puts herself on display for them to assess the damage, they answer yes by moving their heads in synchronized up-and-down motions. She ignores their response and says, "I guess we'd better be going. I'll give you guys a lift to the bus stop this morning. But this is not cool, y'all." The boys gather their book bags and head for the door. Wendy is reaching for her car keys when she takes notice of Eric's shoes.

"Eric," she exclaims, "What happened to the shoes you had me working on this morning?" Eric shrugs his shoulders and innocently responds, "Oh, those ole shoes ... maybe I'll change into those when I get home from school. You like my Air Jordan's, though?!!" Frankie gets a good laugh in as Wendy lets out a loud sigh. She then retorts, "Frick and Frack! That's your new names." She points to each of the boys as she assigns their new names, "You're Frick and you're Frack because you both work so well together in your antics of getting over on your big cousin... yep, Frick and Frack." She closes the door behind them.

More than an hour later, Wendy arrives at school in a bit of a frenzy. The boys missed their bus, so she had to drive them across town in the opposite direction, which took her twenty minutes out of the way. She managed to get them to school on time without incident, however, the shortcut route to her school turned out to be a dead-end road. Wendy doesn't like to be late for school. She needs to be early. She likes to use the extra minutes before the first bell to hide away in the girls' bathroom for some quiet time; this is needed before she starts her day of learning.

She hastily pulls her compact car into one of the parking spaces of the student parking lot. Too bad it's located at least a quarter of a mile from the nearest entrance to the school building. She slams the car in park, cuts off the engine and grabs her book bag from the back floorboard. She jumps out of the car and begins to take the long trek to the school building. When Wendy reaches a full stride, she uses the remote key to lock the car's doors. Upon entrance into the school, she's reminded that today is pep rally day.

The dead giveaway is the crowd of students huddled in the doorway of the gymnasium like cattle being corralled into their stalls and the high school marching band playing the school song intermittently.

Then, there are the squeaky voices of the cheerleaders chanting in unison, "This is Charles T. Turner Tech High, Land of the Tigers. Tigers, go!" This adds to the morning chaos. There she stands, regretting the vigorous jog she's just forced herself to take in the hot morning sun. As her heavy breathing subsides, she begins looking for a quick route to the girls' bathroom. Just then, Amber Clearwater, Wendy's best friend forever, approaches her from behind. She startles Wendy with her greeting.

Amber and Wendy's friendship goes as far back as eighth grade, beginning when Amber, one of the prettiest and most popular girls in the school, rescued Wendy from a horribly humiliating moment in homeroom. A group of their classmates had begun to taunt Wendy, taking advantage of a moment that their teacher had stepped out of the classroom in an emergency. They began to hurl insults at her about her nappy hair, chubby thighs, pimply-faced skin and anything else they could think of in order to torture her. Noticing the tears welling up in Wendy's eyes,

Amber took action. She literally stood between Wendy and the rest of the class and began to hurl insults right back at anyone and everyone; that was until the class took their focus off of Wendy and began to taunt Amber instead.

Needless to say, Amber lost a lot of friends on that day, however, she gained someone who, in turn, rescued her. Amber had been going through her own teenaged problems at home with her mother during this time. At the age of nine and when her brother was just eight, they became fatherless. Amber's father committed suicide during a mental health crisis. Since that time, the morale of her mother and the rest of the family was on a downward slide. Her eighth-grade year was proving to be the worst, as her grades were beginning to slide along with the pristine record of her behavior.

On the day Amber took up for Wendy, the two young ladies bravely sat alone at the same lunch table and instantly became best friends. Amber gained a true friend. That year, she learned what it meant not to feel lonely as they pretty much spent every waking hour together sharing every detail about their lives with each other. They were an odd pair. Their personalities were opposite, but they were each what the other needed during that time. Wendy, being overly emotional in making decisions and highly expressional in her manner of dress and personal image, also had highest scores in the school. That year, she helped Amber get her grades up, and because of Wendy's genius, Amber reached her highest G.P.A ever and has managed to keep it up since. Amber, being more sensible in choices and conservative in dressing, has been able to keep Wendy under impulse control, being the voice of reason when it comes to staying on track with their collective goals.

"Hey, there you are!" says Amber, "I've been looking for you! You want to..." Amber stops mid-sentence, takes a few steps back and begins to examine her friend from head to toe. With a perplexed look on her face, she begins to speak again, "Um, girl, you look like you were in a war zone this morning. What happened to you?!" There's an awkward moment between the two, and then Wendy retorts, "What do you mean?!! Nothing!" By the look on Amber's face, it's clear to Wendy that the answer she just offered her friend doesn't line up with how she looks.

Humiliated, Wendy begins to wipe what appears to be glistening glitter from her forehead, which are actually beads of sweat. Amber narrows her eyes and continues to stare at Wendy; this makes the moment between the two even more awkward. Finally, Amber takes Wendy by the hand and begins to pull her in the direction of the crowd. She begins to bark orders at her, "Well, come on! Let's get in the gymnasium before we have to stand on the sidelines." Wendy pulls her body in the opposite direction, causing Amber to lose her grip on Wendy's hand.

"Um, I'm going to... yeah, head over to the bathroom and, you know, try to pull myself together and, well ..." Amber begins to object, but Wendy cuts her off before she speaks. She says, "You go on ahead and save a seat for me. When I head back to the pep rally, I'll text you for the location." From the determined look on her friend's face, Amber has no choice but to go along with the plan. "Okay," Amber says, "I'll see you in a few." Amber begins to walk away, but then stops in her tracks. She then makes an appeal to her friend, "On second thought, girl, you want me to come with you? Your Afro could use some help..." Wendy objects, "Afro?!! Umm, no. Get our seats. I'll catch up with you." Wendy jets off to the girls' bathroom, dodging through the crowd as Amber does the same in the opposite direction.

Probably because of the pep rally, the normal crowd in the girls' bathroom is pretty scant. Wendy approaches the mirror and immediately understands Amber's comment about her hair. She chuckles as she speaks to herself, "Amber was right. I look like I have an Afro growing around my hairline." From the looks of it, Wendy's hair gel didn't hold up to the humidity that the sun and the heat from her body temperature produced during her jog from her car to the school.

She turns the faucet on, waves her hands briefly under the running water, and begins to swipe the fuzzy hair in an upward motion, beginning where her forehead and hairline meet and just before her carefully braided box braids begin. It doesn't work. Her kinky hair does not surrender its natural curl pattern to the weight of her damp hand. The multiple braids pulled up on the top of her head and twisted into a fashionable messy bun are the perfect style to highlight her dark chocolate skin tone, high cheekbones, ethnic nose and, perfectly plump full lips. She's just regretting not using a stronger hair gel for her edges, but then again, who knew she'd have to go through a, as Amber called it, "war zone" this morning?

She gives up on her hair and turns her attention to the orange stain on her blouse with the same technique she used with her hair. After a moment, her swipes become rubs and the rubbing proves to be pointless. The only change she's made with the orange juice stain is now, it's a wet orange juice stain. She throws her hands up and lets out a frustrated growl. A few girls hanging out in the bathroom react, but then go back to their conversations with one another.

Wendy takes a few steps backwards to get a good look at herself in the full length mirror. Her eyes are astounded at her reflection. First, she sees her 5'9" chubby body taking up all the space in the mirror frame. Next, her eyes fall to the bottom of her pant's legs where the water from this morning's charades with Eric have now dried and formed stains in a pattern that resembles cowgirl fringes. Her eyes move upward to the huge gray circles of sweat under each armpit, and then back to the orange juice stain.

She becomes overwhelmed with emotion as she takes another look at the Afro around her hairline that seems to be swelling by the minute. The reality of how her morning has gone begins to sink in. She speaks out loud, talking to her reflection in the mirror, "Why do I feel like my day is already spent?!! Can it get any worse?!!" Just then, one of the girls in the bathroom answers back, "Honey, from the looks of you, I don't think it could get any worse." Wendy responds with a look that could kill, but the girl is not intimidated, even though she stands a good foot below Wendy in height and weighs probably no more than ninety pounds. Her sassy personality and strong alto voice makes her appear much larger than her actual size, and for certain, much older.

She reaches in her handbag and pulls out a stain remover marker. She offers it to Wendy. "But this might help. I'm Mae, by the way." She extends her other hand for a handshake. Wendy doesn't respond, and Mae nonchalantly pulls her hand away. She then begins to rummage through her bag again. "Oh yeah, I got some hair gel in here somewhere..." Wendy blows her off, speaking to her as she begins to make her way to one of the empty bathroom stalls. "No, thank you...it's just not that serious; you know what I mean?! Um, no offense or anything." Wendy walks into the stall and shuts the door ending the conversation before it begins.

Most of the girls who frequent this bathroom know that Wendy occupies this particular stall every morning before the first period begins. They have all dubbed it her 'office'. Once inside, Wendy proceeds to take care of the agenda of the morning. She pulls out her cell phone and begins to make a call. She clears her throat and waits for the person on the other end to pick up the line. After several rings, someone answers, "Office of admissions. This is Ms. Young. How can I help you?"

Wendy speaks with urgency in her voice, "Oh, hello. Yes ... um, I'm calling because I want to register for this summer's classes, but I'm having trouble doing so online. My student number is 337990, and then all capitals WAB. My name is Wendy Anthelia Brown. And this is like my third time trying to reach your office. After a moment, Ms. Young responds, "Are you sure that's the correct student ID number, Ms. Brown? I don't see anything coming up with this number. What's the last four digits of your social security number? Wendy rattles off the numbers with a little tinge of worry in her voice, "0720."

Ms. Young responds again, "No, nothing. Are you sure you're calling the correct school?" Wendy is frantic now, "What do you mean? Yes, this is the correct school. I have a full academic scholarship to this university." Ms. Young responds, "I'm sorry, but according to our records..." Wendy cuts her off, "What do you mean? I don't have a scholarship?!! I'm holding my award letter in my hands right now... and, I've been accepted into the university ... tell me how could I be accepted into the university and they didn't confirm my full scholarship?!!... I don't have money..."

Ms. Young abruptly cuts her off, "Could you hold the line, please?" Wendy interrupts, "No, don't put me on hold... I got to get to class and ... ugh... she put me on hold! Again!" She hangs up, and before Wendy has an opportunity to call the university again, a loud commotion of teenage voices fills the bathroom. She pauses a moment to wait for the noise to die down. It doesn't; it only gets louder.

Doris, a tall, slender teen, dressed in a snug white button-down blouse and a khaki skirt short enough to reveal a little too much when she sits down, is towering over Mae. Again, Mae is the girl who Wendy just encountered a few minutes earlier. Doris is one of the school's want-to-be 'mean girls'. She's a pretty girl. In truth, she's rather plain-looking except when she's fully made up in her top-of-the-line makeup, which includes false eyelashes, deep purple lipstick and one of her many lace front wigs.

After a full face of make-up and a lace front wig, Doris can pass for a contestant on Tyra Banks, *Next Top Model* show. And she has two disciple-sidekicks, Jackie and Wander, who follow suit. They are just as mean-spirited and they mirror Doris' hair, makeup and wardrobe style choices. If they were as tall as Doris, they could each probably make it on the show as contestants as well. Mae, on the other hand, who is dressed in the same manner, is not quite as glamorous as Doris and her crew. But where she lacks in glamour, she more than makes up for it in cuteness and spunk.

She wears her natural hair swept up to the crown of her head to form a thick, mushroom-shaped Afro puff. Her make-up is subtle and it highlights her caramel skin tone, high cheekbones and large brown eyes just enough so that her natural beauty does not overshadow her spunky personality. Her crumpled skirt and dingy blouse could be a tell-tale sign that Mae is from a low-income household.

Doris and her squad have rushed into the bathroom for the sole purpose of confronting Mae, the new girl, on the subject of boyfriend boundaries. There, in the middle of the bathroom and during Wendy's 'office' hours, Doris reprimands Mae. She says to her,

"Check this out, little girl... I heard you've been easy to my boyfriend... you know he's mine, don't you?!" Jackie and Wander chime in unison, "Yeah, you know he's hers, right?!" Mae stands and stares Doris down with her chin up and shoulders squared, refusing to be intimidated while Doris continues her rant. "I know you think you all that, but you're not... just a note, you're not cute... in fact..." Doris moves even closer to Mae and proceeds to ball up both of her hands into fists. She then raises them to her face as if she's getting ready to box. She continues, "I think we need to teach you a lesson!" She begins to bounce back and forth, shifting her weight between both legs. "Yeah!" Jackie says interrupting, "We need to teach you a lesson because you need to know who's the boss around here since you're the new girl."

By this time, the three girls have formed a semi-circle around Mae and have begun to back her up against the wall. The few girls who are hanging out in the bathroom begin to pull out their cell phones to tape the pending fight. Wander gets in Mae's face, and in the evilest tone that she can muster up, she speaks to Mae, "You just need to kill yourself already!" Doris steps in front of Wander and gives Mae a violent shove to both of her shoulders, causing her to land flush against the wall. Mae regains her balance and suddenly, out of nowhere, cold punches Doris with three successional blows right to her gut.

Just as Wendy tries to escape her 'office' in order to make it to class on time, a full-on fight breaks out. Fists are flying, bodies are moving, and things are getting pretty intense. Refusing to get involved, Wendy tries to slip past the swinging arms in order to make it to the door so that she can escape the bathroom. Meanwhile, Wander has relinquished her position in the brawl in order to serve as the 'look-out' for the others. Wendy looks like she's being forced to do a line dance as she dodges flying fists, determined to look the other way and not get involved. From her perspective, this is a senseless cat fight that is not worth the risk of having to be called to Principal McClain's office for, at the very least, being a witness.

The school bell rings and the fight is raging on with no signs of either side letting up. Wendy concludes that if she wants to make first period class on time, she's going to have to break up this fight; there's just no way around it. She leans in to try and use her body to separate the girls as she admonishes the instigator, "Come on, Doris, that's enough! Leave the poor girl alone. You're just coming for her because she's cuter than you!" "Mind your own business!" Doris snaps back, "I'm the boss here! You need to go kill yourself, fatso!" Wendy snaps back, "Now, do you really think your name calling is going to hurt me?! Please girl, you may have crushed me with that line when I was in eighth grade ... but, I've grown to realize that I'm not fat, I'm slim-thick; hey!" Just then, Wendy gets hit in the mouth by a fist with no name on it.

Frustrated, she becomes a little more committed to breaking up this fight by rough handling Doris. In fact, it could be mistaken that Wendy is actually engaged in the warfare. She then recants with, "Yeah, okay, you don't want none of this, Doris!" At this point, Principal McClain appears in the doorway and her first impulse is to make haste to break up the brawl, but she catches herself. She decides, instead, to take a more unhurried approach.

Principal McClain stands exactly five feet in stature with her arms folded across her body, one inside the other. And with her legs parted, one in front of the other, shifting her bulky body weight to her back leg, she manages to block the door. At first glance, the principal could be mistaken for one of the students. However, at second glance, the fine lines on her forehead, darkened under-eye bags and slightly sagging jowls confirm to the onlooker that she is a much older woman.

She has a growing look of annoyance on her face when Wander notices her and shouts out to the others, "Guys, guys!" Principal McClain quiets her, "Hush Wander. Go right over there and stand still until I tell you otherwise." Wander doesn't comply, but instead begins to wave her hands to get the attention of the brawlers. But by this time, the commotion is so loud that no one hears or sees Wander's efforts to warn them. Wendy has managed to separate the parties, but the physical fight has become a verbal one. Even with the separation, Doris continues to take swings at Mae and spew verbal insults at her.

Meanwhile, Wander makes another attempt to get Doris' attention. She shouts, "Yo, Doris!" Principal McClain turns to Wander, points to the opposite end of the bathroom and speaks in a commanding tone, "NOW!" The Principal's intimidating voice captures the attention of the brawling teenagers just as Wendy, who has become frustrated and more determined to contain Doris, accidentally punches Doris in the nose. Wander shrinks in stature and scurries like a wounded pup to where the Principal has directed her as Doris begins to whine, "Ouch, ouch; my nose. I need a mirror. I think my nose is broken."

Looking at Principal McClain, but talking to the others, Wendy responds, "See, look what you went and did, y'all... I was trying to warn y'all about this very thing. Now Principal McClain, I'm going to let you take it from here... I've got to get to..." Principal McClain cuts Wendy off with much of the same tone as before, "I said quiet! She then turns her attention to Doris, "Come stand right here, Doris!" Holding her nose with one hand and wiping her eyes with the other, Doris begins to make her way towards the principal. Wendy speaks again as she begins to back out of the bathroom door, "But you never said quiet. I think you said, 'Now,' and you were talking to Wander, right?!"

The Principal responds to her with a hint of sarcasm and a lot of correction in her voice, "Now, I'm saying 'Shut up, Wendy!' And where do you think you're going, Wendy?"

Principal McClain then turns her attention back to Doris who has just stood in front of her, and says, "Put your hands down by your sides!" Doris complies and, in doing so, it becomes apparent to all that her nose is not injured and her tears were fake. Wendy continues her conversation with the principal. "Well, I don't want to be late to class so I'm going to go ahead on and..." Principal McClain maintains her control over the situation, responding to Wendy while she exams the length of Doris' dress, "Oh, you're not going to class. Stay right there..."

She measures the relation of Doris' fingertips to her bare thighs, and then speaks again, but this time to Doris. "Doris, you have on your little sister's dress again! And why do you girls need all this makeup?" She takes a step back from the girls and begins to speak to them as a sergeant would his troop, "Alright, girls... I would call you ladies, but you're acting like little girls. Gather up your belongings and follow me." The girls are moving a little too slow for the principal's patience. "Quick, pronto... Now!" She turns to the bystanders and threatens them, "You girls who found these here bathroom shenanigans entertaining enough to be late for class, you're just that! Late for class with no excuse! Take your tardiness with no whining and no tears. Now, get to your classes before I hold you in contempt!" She then turns her attention to the group of girls involved in the fight, "You brawlers, head straight to my office. Don't' try me this morning."

As they begin to move, Wendy mumbles under her breath, "Why is this happening to me? I didn't even do anything but try and keep a fellow classmate from getting hurt today." She looks at Mae with accusation and begins to give her a tongue lashing as the group begins to gather up their backpacks and books. "I don't even know you. Who are you? See, this is what you get when you don't mind your own business. I was minding my own business, then I started minding yours..." Principal McClain cuts Wendy off with a bit of sharpness in her voice, "Wendy, shut up!" They all begin to file out of the bathroom door. Wendy is last to leave before Mrs. McClain. Wendy mumbles under her breath, "What?! I am... dang, so rude..." Maintaining her control over the situation, Principal McClain speaks again as Wendy exits, "I'm going to get the last word, Wendy, ... 'Shut up!'" Left standing alone, the principal takes a quick glance around the empty bathroom before leaving.

About an hour later, inside Principal McClain's office, Wendy sits opposite the principal. Norma Jean McClain is a personable person, but when she has on her 'principal's hat', it's difficult to see her friendliness. Instead, she's often accused of having a 'Napoléon complex'. She runs a tight ship with tremendous authority, despite her small stature. She has served as principal at Charles T. Turner Tech High for the last twenty-five years or so. Now, in her 60's with retirement still far off in the horizon, Principal McClain approaches her day-to-day duty of managing the school with immense care for her students. She has an unending drive to see as many students as possible reach their fullest potential during their high school stay. At the end of the day, she is feared (in a productive way) and loved by all.

From behind her desk, she appears much taller than her actual height. Her eyes pierce at Wendy from over the top of the frame of her glasses as she begins to reprimand her. "Wendy, you look like a kindergartner at the end of their school day. What happened to you? You're going to have to do better than this! You'll be off to college next year, and you should have learned by now that stains on your blouse, uncombed hair and... Lord, have mercy! Yet, here you are sitting before me..." She lets Wendy sit in the humiliation of awkward silence for a moment.

Then she inquires, "Do you know why you're here, Wendy? Wendy loosens up a bit, "You mean like, why I'm here on planet Earth, and like, what my purpose is in life? Wendy tilts her head back as if she's in a deep conversation about life, "You know, I've been thinking about that lately and..." Annoyed, Principal McClain cuts her off, "Wendy! I'm talking about why you're sitting right here in front of me in my office, RIGHT NOW!" She waits for Wendy's response. "Ohhhh, that." Wendy rolls her eyes to the back of her head in order to think of what next to say. "Well, that has nothing to do with me...you see, what had happened was, I was trying to get out of the bathroom so I could get to class... and..."

This still isn't the answer Principal McClain wants to hear, so she interjects, "I'm well aware of what happened between those girls today, Wendy. I'm asking you do you know why you are here?" There is another long awkward pause. Principal McClain relaxes a bit and begins to tap her fingers on her desk comfortably, waiting for an answer. Wendy is not able to bear the awkwardness of the silence. She begins to whine, "What?! It wasn't even my fault. I was trying to break it up... I guess this is what I get for trying to do the right thing. This is exactly why I stay out of peoples' business... I just want to mind my business, do my work, graduate and go to the college of my choice... daaaannnng!"

Principal McClain is unmoved by Wendy's emotions. "It's commendable to rescue the weak, Wendy. It's your mouth that's the problem..." Wendy begins to frantically rummage through her handbag, "My mouth?" She locates a mirror and begins to examine her mouth as she continues, "What's wrong with my mouth?!" Showing signs of growing frustration, Principal McClain turns up her tone a bit, "I'm surprised at you, Wendy! You're a bright young lady. Yet, you are oblivious to your ability to lead ... and therefore, your conduct is atrocious!" "My conduct?! But ... I didn't do anything but try to help a girl who I don't even know. You even said it's commendable..." Principal McClain throws up her hands out of exasperation, "Okay, I'm done..." She then begins to search out her desk. Ignoring Wendy, she locates some forms and begins to write.

Meanwhile, Wendy begins to gather her belongings. She then stands to her feet and proceeds to leave the office. Without looking up, Principal McClain raises her voice. "Hold up. Just where do you think you're going, young lady? I'm not done! Have a seat..." Frustrated, Wendy plops back in her seat. "But, you just said you were done!" The principal sighs at Wendy's attitude. "Wendy, are you really that... you're kidding me right, come on... ?!" She finishes the paperwork and presents it to Wendy. "It pains me to do this, but Wendy, as of now, I'm giving you a four-day suspension from school..." Flabbergasted, Wendy objects, "What? Why?" But Principal McClain continues, "... along with all the other girls involved in today's fiasco."

Wendy's voice begins to crack, "I didn't even do nothing..." The principal continues, "... So, for the rest of the week, you are released from all your classes. I encourage you to take this time to think about why..." With a horrid look on her face, Wendy accepts the paperwork, "This is so unfair. I have never ever been suspended from school... in all my life." She begins to pinch herself, "Oh, my gosh, this is what it feels like to be a high school 'burn-out' ..." Principal McClain gives Wendy a side-eyed glare before continuing to give her instructions, "When you return to school next week, you will be assigned to a detention project of my choice until the end of the year. Is this clear?" "Wait, detention, project till the end of the year!?! ..." Wendy looks heavenward, "God, why? Am I cursed?"

Unmoved by Wendy's dramatic display, Principal McClain continues, "You may finish out this school day, but make sure to get your homework assignments for the rest of the week, Wendy... because, you are not allowed back on school property until Monday. Is that clear?" Wendy is almost in tears,

"Why do I feel like a criminal right now?!" Just then, the school bell rings. The principal says on cue, "Ooooh, look at that! Saved by the bell! Bye." She points to the door, and with a curt smile on her face, waves goodbye as Wendy drags herself out of the office and closes the door.

After Wendy leaves, the principal exchanges her serious facial expression for a mischievous one as she picks up her desk phone. "Yes, hello. Barbara? Two words, one person... Wendy Brown. Yes, girl. I just gave her a suspension for the rest of the week. I know... but, it's not going to go on her record. I have a plan. Has she joined any extracurricular activities in this year or last? That's what I thought! I don't think that, in the going on four years now, she's been involved in much! This girl is full of potential. I think she could make a great leader someday, but she just doesn't seem to want to get involved with much or take anything serious. I'll just meet with you directly after the last period. I've got a plan and I need your help. Okay, thanks. See you then."

Hours later, Wendy has managed to make it through the school day. She sits in her last period class barely able to pay attention. Her anxious thoughts are getting the best of her as the reality of having been suspended from school sets in. Mrs. Stance, a thirty-something petite woman, dressed conservatively in a blush pink pull-over sweater and black slacks, stands in the front of a full, Journalism 201 class. She begins to wrap up her lecture. "We have about ten minutes left in class, so stop what you're doing everyone. We need to have a quick meeting about the yearbook for this year."

She waits a moment while the class complies before resuming. "Okay, so most of you know this ... well actually, if you're in this class, you all know that the Journalism class is responsible for gathering content, doing the layout and editing for the school's yearbook every year. We would have to get started this semester if we want a terrific finished project... so if..." She stops to answer a student's raised hand, but he begins to speak before she calls upon him to do so. He speaks in a hurried kind of way, "We need an editor-in-chief. We have to choose an editor-in-chief before we can get started ..." There is a small whispering eruption throughout the class.

Brandon, a handsome, neatly dressed young man, wearing gold, wire-rimmed circled glasses that seem to unintentionally go with his nerdy personality, stops talking and acknowledges the awkward giggles, gasps and interjections. But, he's not deterred from his point, "What?! Those are the rules..." He turns to Mrs. Stance, "Can I serve this year as editor-in-chief? I have some really good ideas that I've been mulling around in my head for the last year. I think I got this...." Mrs. Stance responds, "Brandon, pardon me, but I know what the rules are... and I'm sure you have some great ideas." She turns her attention back to the class and continues, "As I was saying, if we want a terrific finished project, then everyone will have to contribute because, look around you; this class is the yearbook club. So, beginning next week Monday, you are required to stay after school for our first yearbook club meeting, at which time I will announce who will be this year's editor-in-chief." Another student, Chrissy, raises her hand and Mrs. Stance gives her permission to speak with a slight head gesture. "So, Mrs. Stance, what if you're not able to stay after school on Mondays? Does this mean you're exempt from participating?" Mrs. Stance puts her hands on her hips as she exclaims, "Let me be clear—every student that signed up for this class was well aware of the fact that staying after school to work on the yearbook is a requirement. And each of you confirmed you knew this when you signed up. The student who does not comply will face detention ..."

Chrissy interjects, "But, I don't have a ride home... and ..." "Not my problem," Mrs. Stance says. Addressing the rest of the class, she continues, "Figure it out. It's too late to drop this class without penalty... and besides, all the elective classes are filled to the brim, honey..." Wendy blurts out her objection as other students begin to whine and complain, "But um, see... that was going to be my point... I just got thrown in this class. The elective that I wanted to take and my second choice were filled up, so no offense, Mrs. Stance, I didn't make plans to join the yearbook club... I was planning on dropping this class ..."

Brandon cuts her off, "How could you not want to be in this class...?" Out of growing frustration and fear of losing control over her class, Mrs. Stance harshly brandishes Brandon, "Okay, Brandon, raise your hand if you need to say something. And next time, make sure it's relevant." She then addresses Wendy, "Ms. Brown. Not my problem. Make a plan to be here or else face detention. Okay class, we are about out of time. Tomorrow, we will finish up on the procedure of setting interview appointments with adults..." At this, the last period school bell rings and Mrs. Stance lets out a loud sigh. "Alright, see you all tomorrow."

The students begin to file out of the class. Brandon and Wendy make their way to Mrs. Stance. Chrissy approaches Wendy, so Brandon arrives first to Mrs. Stance. Chrissy politely taps Wendy on the shoulder, "Wendy, is it? Can I talk to you for a moment?... Um, you think you can give me a ride home on Mondays... starting next week? Umm, I take the city bus and ..." Wendy closes her eyes and drops her head as she cuts Chrissy short, "Ump, no. Not my problem... I don't even know you..." Chrissy walks away looking embarrassed and stressed out.

Wendy approaches Mrs. Stance just as Brandon begins to speak, "So, Mrs. Stance, I was serious about volunteering to be the editor-in-chief this year. As you know, I'm more than qualified to handle the position... here's my resume." Mrs. Stance tries to keep her frustration hidden by plastering a big plastic smile on her face. "Brandon, as I've stated before, I will be making that decision on Monday." She hands his resume back to him and continues with the same fake smile, "I admire your eagerness, but this position doesn't require a resume, darling." There is an awkward moment. Her smile fades as Mrs. Stance is expecting Brandon to excuse himself, but realizing that she needs to dismiss him, she resumes with the same pretentious smile, "Okay, bye now." Frustrated,

Brandon leaves as Wendy begins, "Mrs. Stance, umm... Principal McClain...um, I was suspended this morning for the rest of the week and ..." Mrs. Stance interrupts, "I know." Wendy raises her eyebrows and Mrs. Stance corrects herself, "I mean. Uh, you were? Whatever for?" Wendy answers under her breath, "For no reason that was good enough!" She speaks a little louder as she continues, "Anyway, I need to get any assignments and lessons that I'll miss." Mrs. Stance can tell that Wendy is a little embarrassed about having to ask for assignments and such.

Her instinct is to let Wendy know that it's all a big scam, but instead, she tries to show her a little sympathy, "Okay, sure. I'll email them to your student email account. You'll have them first thing in the morning. Well, have a good... or ... productive rest of the week. See you on Monday." Wendy leaves with her head hung low just as Savannah enters the classroom with a big smile on her face and carrying a small tray of food. She notices Wendy, "Hey, hey, hey! What's going on, Wendy? Is everything okay? Wendy whines back, "Nooooo.... but I'll be okay. Hello, Ms. Savannah." She halfheartedly greets Savannah with a hug, and then hurriedly leaves the classroom.

Mrs. Stance is gathering her computer bag and handbag when she notices Savannah. "Oh, hello Savannah. Can you remind Marguerite of the permanent schedule change, which begins next week, Monday? So, as we discussed earlier, we can kindly move you all to another classroom or... another day even..." Savannah politely cuts her off, "She's put everyone on notice. Beginning Monday, we'll be pushing back our meeting time, since none of us want to be in Mr. White's classroom... it's so dark and eerie there." She steps back, takes a deep breath and slowly exhales before saying, "There's something special about the atmosphere of this classroom."

Mrs. Stance stops what she's doing for a moment to emphasize her response to Savannah's last comment about her classroom. "The special thing about the atmosphere? It's called prayer... and you know I be slinging my oil every morning before school begins. I be throwing down in here..." Savannah chuckles at this as she joins in the humor, "I know you do... the way you be going in at church, girl... I know the demons have to get to running time your feet hit this campus..." They slap each other's hands as Mrs. Stance continues, "You better know it! Ain't nobody playing with the devil. We have some highly gifted kids in this school, and I'm on a mission to make sure no devil from hell steals their destiny." She goes back to gathering her things, but then stops to ask Savannah a question.

"Now, Wendy Brown is your niece, right? She is one of those gifted kids..." Savannah cuts her off to correct her, "No, she's not my niece, but she might as well be. She and my niece, Amber, Bethany's daughter, are best friends.... those two are like two peas in a pod... like sisters. Is there something wrong?" Just then a small group of adults begin to stream into the classroom and Mrs. Stance realizes that she needs to cut their conversation short in order to accommodate the upcoming Overcomers' Substance Abuse meeting. "Oh, nothing serious. We'll talk. Let me get out of your way. It looks like your meeting will be starting soon. See you next time." Mrs. Stance exits her classroom as Principal McClain meets her in the hallway. They walk off in deep discussion.

# Chapter Two

## Overcomers Anonymous

The group of people begin to greet one another as they help themselves to the snacks. Savannah and a few others begin to arrange the chairs in a circle. Alexis, a chubby thirty-year-old with a gorgeous face and dark curly hair, is the first to speak. "I'm glad to be here tonight because I had a horrible day." Marguerite, a slightly older Spanish woman in her forties, neatly dressed in a business suit and heels, chimes in. She speaks clear English with a Spanish accent. "I did as well..." Savannah speaks from across the room, "Must be something in the air..."

Adding to the current conversation, Bill approaches Savannah, and speaking with an obnoxious tone, says, "Well, there's nothing like a good meeting to chase the blues away..." He leans a little too close to Savannah and she gets a good look at his bloodshot eyes and a good whiff of his alcohol-soaked breath. She's about to call him out when Joseph, a slight man, dressed in a well-made tailored business suit and looking to be in his early fifties, approaches them.

He stops and plants his feet exactly between Savannah and Bill, and with a look of bewilderment on his face, makes direct eye contact with Bill.

He extends his hand toward him and begins to speak with the absence of confidence as they shake hands. "Hello, I suppose I'm in the right place. This is ..." He looks over one of his shoulders and then the other one. Then, he leans in close to Bill and whispers, "That place, right?!" Well, Bill finds a bit of humor in Joseph's need for secrecy, so he proceeds with the same level of secrecy. He leans into Joseph's ear and whispers back, "You are correct sir. This is that place." Then, he speaks louder, startling Joseph, "But it's not a secret." Bill begins to indulge in an exaggerated laugh largely brought on by the level of his tipsiness.

When he pulls himself together, he says, "You can say it, you know... it's a recovery group meeting .... and we are all in this together bro, you know... alcoholics and druggies... ... Bill is my name." He releases his hand grip with Joseph and waits for Joseph to respond. Finally, Joseph does respond in the same shaky voice as before, "Oh, my name... are we allowed to give our names, or... oh, I see ... a code name, right?!" Bill shakes his head 'no' and begins again to poke fun at Joseph. But Savannah, who's been observing the conversation, steps in. She berates Bill with her eyes, then turns to Joseph to connect with him and calm him down, but before she gets the opportunity to speak, Marguerite intervenes.

She speaks with a calm voice, almost funeral home like, "Hello I'm Marguerite, group chairperson ... we encourage first names only. These 'Anonymous' meetings are not secret meetings... just anonymous in nature...and of course, you do know that this particular group is Christ-centered..." She can see that he's still a little hesitant and confused, so she continues in a much happier and more upbeat tone, "Well, relax. You'll catch on... I can show you, uh; what is your name, sir?" He responds with a timid voice, "Oh, right... My name—Joseph... Joseph Sparks... oops... no last names, only first names... Oh gosh, I can't take that back... oh, just forget the last name, will you... just poof," he throws his hands up with nervous energy as to do some kind of magic trick, "...forget that last name ..."

He lets out another nervous giggle, and with wide eyes, Marguerite attempts to mend this painful moment, "Alrighty, let's just get you settled into a front row seat ... and would you like coffee and a brownie beforehand?! Savannah, can you help Joseph with snacks and a seat? Thank you." Savannah begins to pour coffee for him. Afterwards, she grabs a plate, hastily places a brownie on it and beckons him to follow her to a seat. Joseph complies, and as they scurry to a seat, Bill hands Marguerite a folded piece of paper. Speaking in the same tipsy tone, he says, "Ms. Marguerite, you think you can go ahead and sign this now?"

She lets out a sigh. Then, without even looking at the paper, she sternly responds, "Now Bill, I told you last week... you're on court order to attend these meetings, and I will not be party to you ducking out before we end... signature after we adjourn, and not a minute before!" She walks away, leaving him stunned and holding the crumpled paper. "Well, alright then, Madame chairperson." After a moment, he snatches a brownie from the platter and regains his composure before taking a seat in the circle of chairs.

A few moments later when everyone has settled, Marguerite rises from her seat, steps into the middle of the circle and begins to greet the small crowd. "Hello everyone, I'm Marguerite and I'm an overcomer. We're just about ready to begin, so Savannah, why don't you give the opening statement?" Savannah stands and begins to speak, "Welcome everyone, I'm Savannah and I have overcome addictions. For you new over- comers, this is a 12-step meeting, which means – the focus is on some aspect of the twelve steps from the Big Book, Christ-centered, of course. You are not required to contribute to today's discussion. However, if you should want to, keep your comments orderly, to the point, be brief and take a seat. Okay?!" She snaps her finger, and then her neck as she energetically takes her seat.

Afterwards, Marguerite continues from where she's sitting, "Okay. Today's topic is step number four." She begins to read from a big blue book with a hardcover, "We made a searching and fearless moral inventory of ourselves." She closes the book and addresses the group, "Okay, let's stand as we recite the serenity prayer together." Everyone stands, with Bill being the last one to rise to his feet, as they all recite the prayer in unison, "God grant me the serenity to accept the things I cannot change, courage to change the things I can, and wisdom to know the difference. Amen." As they take their seats again, Marguerite begins to speak, but this time, with an after thought. "Okay, before we get into a discussion about step number four, I think we should review the first three steps for the new faces."

She picks up the big blue book again, turns the pages, and stops when she's found the page she needs. She then begins reciting step one. "Step one. We admitted we were powerless over alcohol and drugs—that our lives had become unmanageable." Step two is, we came to believe that a Power greater than ourselves could restore us to sanity. And step three reads, 'Made a decision to turn our will and our lives over to the care of God as we understood Him.' I'm opening up the floor for discussion of these three steps. Who has something to say about step one?"

After a brief moment, Alexis takes a quick look around the circle, sees that no one is budging, and begins to speak up, "Simply put, I had to accept the fact that me and Mary Jane; that's weed for those of you who don't know her; though we got along really well at first, she really disrupted my life. Step one, for me, was life-changing and actually liberating. You see, I'm the type that if I'm curious, I'm going to try it... and if I like it, I'm going to indulge in it... again and again and again." She blurts out a corny laugh at her own joke. When she notices that no one got the joke, she resumes sharing, "See, I met her in high school. She seemed to help me calm down and focus. At the time of our meeting, she was a much-welcomed friend. Back then, a lot was happening in my life. My older sister got married and moved out. She was my best friend. Shortly afterwards, a younger cousin moved in, and she became my worst nightmare. Smoking a blunt every now and again helped me mellow out and better cope with anger issues. Oh yeah, she—Mary Jane, not my younger cousin—helped me get through high school honor classes with flying colors. But, by the time I finished grad school, Mary Jane had me walking around comatose, like the walking dead. Getting the revelation that I had a problem was a long time coming. After my eyes were opened, admitting it came quickly. You ever read that scripture in the Bible, 'Whatever you offer yourself to, that's what you will eventually become enslaved to?"

David quickly chimes in with the correct scriptural reference, "Romans 6:16." Then, he continues, "Well, I had to admit complete defeat, even when I realized that my alcohol problem had a hold on me. I was reluctant to admit it out loud because... then it would become real... but, I could no longer ignore the fact that I couldn't have just one drink. If I had one, I had them all ... and well, the 'all' factor is what ruined my life, stole my family, and tricked me into believing that

I was in control. Well, let's just say, I became a slave; I was in bondage to alcohol." After a moment of silence, Savannah thoughtfully speaks; she simply says, "Powerless... no power to manage our own lives."

Alexis energetically resumes her thoughts, "Yes! See, I thought I could handle the weed, but after a while, I couldn't have weed without alcohol and alcohol without the weed... it was insane, as if I had lost my own mind—and I didn't sign up for all that... you know what I mean? ... I only signed up for the weed... but she had me in places I never thought I'd be, doing things I never thought I'd do, with people I never thought I'd be doing it with ... beds I never thought..." she abruptly stops for a second or two, then continues, "... well, that's another meeting... Mary Jane just turned out to be so wicked... so yeah, I was ready to admit defeat..."

After another moment of silence, Savannah begins to share part of her story. She recites step two. "Came to believe a power greater than ourselves could restore us to sanity. Drug of choice? Cocaine was my euphoric; it helped me to cope ... then, it became the monkey on my back! When I decided that I didn't want to die in that condition, I couldn't find the strength within myself to break free ... I wanted to, but I was powerless..." Talking a bit too loud as if he's trying to talk over loud music in order to be heard, Bill very rudely cuts Savannah off. He says mockingly, "Powerless?!... All it takes is self will, gosh darn, y'all. If a person wants to stop drinking... that is 'wants" being the operative word... all they have to do is stop drinking or using drugs or whatever. Period! End of story."

Savannah, ignoring meeting rules, addresses Bill directly, "If you don't mind Bill, tell me why you're here again?" He rolls his eyes, throws his arms up, and grudgingly shrugs his shoulders at Savannah. "Court ordered, Savannah. You know that..." She answers him in a condescending way, "Oh, because I keep thinking it has something to do with WHY the judge saw fit to make attending these meetings mandatory... that's all." He snaps back at her, "Look now, don't go there with me..." Savannah ignores him and continues to offend him, "... and now this is your second time?! Oh, but my bad..."

Feeling a little defeated and very much disrespected, he snaps back yet again, "These meetings and the people at these meetings make you want to drink..." Refusing to let up off him, she drives the pin in his inflated ego with a huge dose of sarcasm, "Exactly my point! It's everyone else's fault..." Marguerite, who has been secretly enjoying the 'Bill roast' finally comes to his rescue, rebuking Savannah, "Okay, you two. Can we maintain some semblance of order here? Savannah, you know better!" Savannah laughs as she says something inaudible.

As the discreet laughter dies down and everyone has a moment to regain their composure and perspective, David shares his thoughts. "I'm over twenty years sober... that's a long time to some of you, but once I recognized the need to get sober, it took me about five years of trying to turn my life over to the care of God... you know. I was hitting and missing. One day, I maintained sobriety and the next day, I would convince myself that I was in control. I had a drink, and if I had one drink, I had them all... that's the definition of step two—insanity—knowing something's bad for you, but you keep indulging, expecting different results. Albert Einstein said something to that effect. I had a substance abuse problem because I had a 'self-will' problem. I guess I figured that I had to maintain some control over my life in order to maintain my manhood. You know the title of that song... Jesus, Take the Wheel. I needed to learn how to truly 'let go and let God,' turning my total life over to His care. By the way, that's step three, you know."

"Yep, I know what you mean" Marguerite says, "For me, trying to get sober on my own was like trying to row a boat against the stream... you can row hard and long... but sooner or later, the strength of the current will take you out in a blink of an eye. Overpowered, you're back where you started from. Oh, it will take a power greater than yourself..." It's a sobering thought that Marguerite just shared, and the people in the meeting begin to ponder it. After a moment, David blurts out another Bible scripture, "Romans 10:13, "For whosoever shall call upon the name of the Lord shall be saved."

David looks around the circle of overcomers, then fixes his eyes on Bill before he continues, "Some of us won't call on Him because we are loyal to a loveless relationship; the 'taskmaster' with his drugs, alcohol, food, sex... you fill in the blank." Savannah chimes in, "Yeah, one-sided love affair. Make that clear, David, will you? The devil, with his cocaine and crack pipe, did not love me..." "If we can't grasp that there is a sufficient love that will rescue us," David explains, "... it's because we are anesthetized in bondage... so even when we get sick and tired of being sick and tired, we cling to what's familiar, rather than take a chance on love. But when we feel defeated and helpless…, the one thing we don't want to do is pretend we don't have a problem… trust me, I spent a lifetime in a loveless affair with heroin because I didn't think the love of God would be enough…"

Sucking her teeth and shaking her head, Alexis lifts a hand as she points one finger upwards and begins, as if she's in the middle of preaching a fiery sermon, "You must believe and receive… He that calls upon the Lord shall be saved! Can I get an Amen?!…" She abruptly stops, drops her preachy voice and then continues, "Hey, does that scripture apply to everyday use? I mean, I be calling upon the Lord all the day long…. these people at work… they are trying to kill me…" With this, there is a welcomed change in the overall mood in the meeting. The atmosphere becomes a little lighter as Savannah inquires of Alexis, "Where do you work again?"

Alexis answers with attitude, "At the telephone company—AB&C Call Center… and it's a conspiracy, I swear." Savannah asks, "Oh, you a supervisor there?" Alexis answers with less of an attitude and more of embarrassment, "No, I'm a customer service agent..." Savannah says, "Oh, I thought you..." and Alexis finishes her sentence, "... had a real job?! I did! I had a really good job... let's just say that one day, I had to vacate the premises ... in a hurry. But that's another meeting... so now, here I am a grown woman working a job for minimum wages ... teenagers making more money than me... a girl nineteen-years old thinks she's the boss of me..."

Joseph, who has been listening intently and even taking notes throughout the meeting, finally works up enough courage to speak. He apologetically says, "Well, if she's your manager or supervisor, she is the boss of you. I own a call center, so I know how they work..." Alexis chuckles, but not at what he's said, but more so at what she's getting ready to say. "Well sir, I hope you don't run it like AB&C runs theirs. I used to think AB&C stood for American Broadband and Communications until I started working there..." Joseph objects, "Pardon me, but that is what it stands for, right?!"

Alexis explains, "Sir, work there for about two weeks! You'll find that they've been lying to you—to all of us ... it stands for All Broke Colored's ... referring to both the employees and the customers... G to the H, to the ETTO... GHETTO! Any given day I'm liable to lose my sobriety. I be calling on the Lord... Jesus, hold it down!" She looks upwards and begins to talk to the Lord, "Lord, I hope you don't get tired of me!" She looks back at Joseph and continues, "Like today is Monday. I dubbed it Mood day..." Joseph gives a warm smile to Alexis as he shows empathy to her, "Oh, you have to deal with a lot of crazy customers with bad moods... I get it!"

"No," she corrects him and explains what she means. "A lot of customers have to deal with a lot of crazy me and my bad moods..." The group begins to laugh as Alexis takes a moment to adjust herself in her chair, and then continues, "It seems like on Mondays, I get all the customers who have a tendency to get on my last nerve. Like today, one lady, just as rude as all get out... couldn't listen to anything I had to say. See, she thought she had game. She didn't want to pay her bill, so she plotted. She insisted that I cut her phone service off because she 'didn't use all that overage in data.'" Alexis quickly puts her hand to her ear as if she's talking on the phone.
She proceeds to act out the conversation, interchanging her voice, becoming the customer at times. She says, in a very polite, professional voice, "Ma'am, does anyone live with you?"
"No."

'Does anyone have access to your phone?'
'No.'
'Lady!... You used the data!'
She had the nerve to raise her voice, cuss me out, and demand that I turn the service off... 'NOW!' she yells at me. Ma'am, okay, let me put that order in for you, ... oh, she screaming at me... 'NOW!'"
Alexis looks at her fellow overcomers, and with the most mischievous grin on her face, she says, "Ask me what I did!" Savannah says, "Girl, what did you do?" Alexis answers, returning to her preachy voice and with a sense of gratification, "Yet, while she was still speaking... I cut her service off..." She laughs a vindicating laugh that makes others laugh along with her. Even Joseph gets a nervous chuckle out.

Determined to make the moment a teaching one, David speaks directly to Alexis, "You know, you really need to work on the fruit of the Spirit. Have you ever thought that just maybe the reason you're at that job is because God is using it to show you your faults, and He's humbling you? Here's a secret... the sooner you acquiesce, the sooner He'll promote or restore you." Her laughter fades into a smile, and then a half-smile, until it's completely gone. She speaks with a sober and humble attitude, "I guess I do know that, but it's so hard. Y'all better be careful what you ask for. I asked God to change me. But, here's the truth, I didn't think I was that bad!" She laughs really loud and continues, "The Lord have me on lock down. I do know it's Him working on me... He's working out the fruit of patience."

David deliberately looks at Alexis side-eyed and clears his throat. Alexis gets the point and nervously laughs as she responds, "Okay, with a lot of those fruits... everything from love, joy, and all the way to self-control..." She looks at David, and then continues, "looooong suffering..." She giggles, and then gets serious again, "But man, some days, I'm so tempted to smoke me a blunt... before I step into the workplace. Seriously! And another at lunch and another on my way home in order to shake off the crazy... only thing that stops me is when I run that story all the way to the end... and I see that 'the end' of that story is not a happy one. Right?!"

They all enjoy a moment of silence as they allow themselves to dwell on what would be the tragic end to their own stories if they allowed themselves to pick up their vices again. Then Marguerite speaks up, "Right?! It doesn't look so pretty. I remember where I came from ... how unmanageable my life really was. This is my 'go to' reminder when I'm feeling tempted. I remind myself that alcohol defeated me, and then I rerun the tape back on some of those not so enjoyable scenes..." Alexis adds a bit of affirmation to her own circumstance, "Yep, this job isn't much, but it makes me feel alive... that and Jesus..."

Savannah goes back to an earlier point that Alexis made. She begins to reflect on her own life, "Well, I knew I was THAT bad... but I played the blame game ... I blamed my alcoholic mother, my no-show daddy, the system... and all the other folks who did me wrong. It started going well with me the day I acknowledged to God my part in all of it. Really. I finally came to terms and admitted to myself, and then to God... I chose to pick that crack pipe up, no matter the reasons why ... I did that. That's where I had to start with God and not with excuses. Excuses are like buttholes; everyone has one." "Yes!" Alexis says, "I was convinced that nothing was my fault."

"I had a sense of entitlement, I suppose, and an excuse for everything. I smoked because people drove me to smoke. I needed to mellow out, because people and their ways got me all wound up. And my attitude was, I expected people to do for me, especially my family. After all, they owe me... right?! I used to really believe the hype... If they're in a better position, they should help a sister out! What does it matter if I live with them or come over and eat every day? They have to pay their mortgage either way! They have to cook for their family; what's another mouth to feed?! One person can't possibly make that big of a difference, right?!" In a drunken slur, Bill blurts out "Amen! Yeah, you better preach, sister! I'm trying to tell them, but they don't want to listen. Finally, someone who understands." Apparently, Bill is the only one in the room who doesn't get Alexis' sarcasm. They all stare at Bill with wide eyes, waiting for him to acknowledge that he was joking. It doesn't happen, so Alexis continues without acknowledging Bill's input.

She says, "I moved in with that cousin who moved in with us. Everything was going well, but when I quit my job, she had the nerve to lock me out AND change the locks." She takes a moment to laugh at her own absurdity. "I lived with my sister and her family until I was asked to leave. Then, I lived with my widowed mother for the last three years of her life." She shifts to a soberer mood as she recants an unpleasant reality. "She was self-sufficient and doing okay, managing her poor health to where she eventually became stable. Then, I moved in. I thought her house was my refuge, a place to lay my head until I felt like getting up and getting back on my feet.

I did what I wanted to do and took what I needed to take. It wasn't long after she passed that I found myself homeless. The house I was expecting to inherit went back to the bank. The life that I had been imposing on was bankrupt, including her bank account. I had burned all my bridges with family. I found myself in a homeless shelter... humiliated. When I finally got sober, I was living out of my car and barely holding on. I was faced with myself. Sobriety has a way of helping you face yourself... there is no escaping you." Alexis flashes a quick look at Bill, then continues. "I mean, that is if you truly want sobriety and to stay sober..."

After an appropriate length of time, Marguerite begins to close the meeting. "Well, what a sobering thought, Alexis. I think we are ready to discuss step four now, but we are out of time. She turns her attention to Bill. "Bill, to give us something to think on for our next meeting, can you read step four out loud for us, please, and elaborate?" Bill reluctantly rises to his feet and walks to the front of the room where the big blue book is. He picks it up and begins to read from it. *"Made a searching and fearless moral inventory of ourselves."* He closes the book, places it back on the table, and begins to share, "This is the step where you have to begin looking at your faults, I guess...

See here's the problem with this step for me... it's not my fault..."

## Chapter Three

## Secrets

It's Monday evening, the official evening before the first day of Wendy's suspension from school, and she and Amber are sitting on her living room sofa talking. Wendy is looking defeated as Amber speaks to her, "It really is hard to believe that Principal McClain threw you out of school." Wendy speaks with a whiny voice, "Amber, you make it sound so devastating. I mean, it is devastating, but you make it sound... devastating..." Amber reaffirms Wendy's situation, "Yeah, it is pretty devastating." At this last comment, Wendy gives Amber a side-eye stare, and then there is a bit of an uncomfortable silence in the room before Amber speaks again.

She says, "I feel like you're Job in the Bible and I'm one of his friends who comes to comfort him, but just sits in silence with nothing to say..." There's silence again. Then Amber continues, "So, what are you going to do for the rest of the week? Girl, you better tell your mom..." Frustrated and annoyed, Wendy responds, "I thought you were going to sit in silence with nothing to say?!..." At this remark, Amber gives Wendy a side-eye stare. She patiently waits for an answer with her eyes remaining fixed on her best friend. Wendy finally responds with a sigh, "I guess, hide out in the library and sulk. Oh yeah, take the boys to school, and then go to the library and sulk. Lord forbid they find out. No secret is safe with Frick and Frack." "Who is 'Frick and Frack?" Amber asks. "Frankie and Eric... long story for another time," says Wendy.

They both stop talking and begin to follow Pop-Pop with their eyes as he appears from down the hall. He slowly strolls pass where the girls are sitting in the living room as he continues to make his way towards the kitchen. He stops at the refrigerator, opens the door and has a look inside. After this, he closes the door to the fridge as if he's forgotten what he wanted. He turns and slowly makes his way to the living area, where he stops in front of the girls and says to no one in particular, "There are no secrets that time does not reveal." He continues to make his way down the hall, adding, "The dramatist, Jean Racine, said that," just before he disappears into his bedroom. Wide-eyed, the girls remain quiet for a moment. Then, Amber says, "There's no way he heard us. Pop-Pop is spooky." Nonchalantly, Wendy responds, "I thought it was just me; it happens all the time." Amber continues to stare at Wendy with wide eyes.

But, after a moment, Wendy continues, "Oh yeah, and then there is the issue of my admissions to the University ... I don't have an academic scholarship according to them... I'm not worried or anything, It's just that it's nerve-wrecking." Before Amber can probe Wendy about the issues surrounding her scholarship and university admission, Martha Lee Brown, Wendy's mother, arrives home. As she appears from behind the front door, she's visibly upset, but she's trying hard to conceal it.

Martha Lee is a hard-working and gentle woman who loves her daughter. By trade, she's a hairdresser, and a good one at that. In fact, it's something she's been doing practically all her life. Cosmetology school was just an after thought—a way to officially start her brand and take care of her newborn. After school, when Wendy turned one, she leased a small space in the west wing of a downtown building, and the rest is history. Shortly after that, while still in her thirties, she was able to buy a building, and today, she owns one of the largest salons within a thirty-mile radius.

Her business took off so fast that Martha Lee was able to purchase the very home they live in today just after Wendy began grade school. Martha Lee has always been a humble woman. Never married, single mom, choosing to live a modest life, not out of necessity, but because of her humble nature. She always gave God credit for all of her good fortunes. But, the one thing she takes pride in is having been able to provide stability for her only child for all these years. Because of stability, Wendy was shielded from some of the heartaches she herself had to endure as a young woman.

Upon seeing Wendy and Amber sitting in the living room, Martha Lee lingers at the door for a moment in order to swallow her emotions before she greets them. "Oh, hi Amber. How is everyone? It's so unusual for y'all to be home so early after school." She begins to approach the girls. "Wendy, daughter, how was your day?" Wendy gives Amber a brief look of warning to keep her secret before she stands to greet her mom. Martha Lee gives her daughter a quick kiss on the cheek and a lingering hug, all the while thinking of a way to get the girls out of the house; that is, at least until she can digest the emotions she's just swallowed.

"You know, I didn't get a chance to even think about dinner for tonight." Martha Lee reaches inside her purse, pulls cash out, and puts it in her daughter's hand just as Gurley barges in from her bedroom. Hearing the food part of the conversation, Gurley puts her bid in for what they'll have for dinner as she speaks with enthusiasm. "Oh yeah, let's have pizza from Pistachios tonight. Order the six-piece chipotle chicken wings as well, but order them just before you get ready to leave... I like 'em nice and hot... right out of the oven... Oh yeah, and bring home a large pizza for the boys' lunch tomorrow. You know they can eat pizza cold." She takes a second to laugh, and then completes her order, "... and bring two liters of strawberry soda, and yeah, make that a twelve-piece order of wings for me."

Wendy sticks her hand out signaling for Gurley to put money in it. Gurley slaps her empty hand into Wendy's empty hand and tries to continue with her dinner order. But Wendy obnoxiously keeps her hand out, almost in Gurley's face ready for her to pay up. Gurley pushes Wendy's hand away and begins to defend herself, "Now, you know Mamma gave you enough money for me... girl, you trying to be slick..." Wendy cuts her off while Amber begins to chuckle at the shenanigans of Wendy's aunt. "She's your sister...

AUNTIE, ... she's MY mother... and I don't..." Martha Lee cuts in by clearing her throat and signaling to her daughter to "let the matter go." She reaches into her bag for more money. She then hands it to Wendy.

Wendy speaks under her breath as she and Amber gather themselves to leave. She says, "The guest that just won't leave..." As they open the front door to leave, Mr. Eugene Jean is standing in front of the door, ready to knock. The girls greet him as they leave. Mr. Jean steps through the open door. "Now, Mr. Jean, I wasn't counting on having any company tonight," Martha Lee says sternly. There is an awkward moment between the three. Gurley finally realizes that she needs to excuse herself. "Oh, I'll be in my room... call me when the food gets here..."

Eugene Jean has always been sort of an enigma to the family, especially to Martha Lee, more than what she's been willing to admit to herself since she met him all those years ago. Back then, when he literally slipped into their lives, Wendy was just a few months old. Martha Lee had just joined the beauty academy, pursuing her license in cosmetology. Mr. Jean was and still is a chef in one of the most celebrated restaurants in the area. Back then, he was also a cooking instructor by night. He taught culinary arts in the building adjacent to the beauty school that Martha Lee attended.

One rainy night after her class, Martha Lee was wrestling with Wendy's clunky stroller in order to fit it into her compact car. Mr. Jean happened to be walking to his bus stop when he noticed her struggling. Being the gentleman that he is, he came running to her rescue, but slipped and fell into a huge water puddle before he could help. Martha Lee managed to fit the stroller in the car as she always had, but Mr. Jean was soaked from head to toe. There they were, standing in the rain.

After shaking off his embarrassment of having fallen short as a knight in shining armor, he introduced himself as "The Mr. Eugene Jean, a chef and culinary instructor." Martha Lee got such a big kick out of the rather formal introduction of himself that she followed suit. She introduced herself in the same manner, "Ms. Martha Lee Brown, 'The' up and coming hair and beauty expert." They both got a good chuckle from this, and afterwards, she insisted on rescuing him from the rain. He turned down her offer to drive him home, and instead, talked her into a cup of coffee at the diner down the street. So, the three of them waited out the rain over a cup of coffee that evening.

And till this day, Mr. and Ms. has been their expression of endearment for one another.

Almost ten years her senior, Martha Lee found him charming, handsome, and she especially appreciated his over-the-top chivalry while having coffee with him. She appreciated his chivalry enough to accept his dinner invitation for the following week and every week pretty much after that week until this day. Admittedly, there has been one thing about him that has always put Martha Lee on edge. The overwhelming air of loneliness he carries with him. It's almost as if he deliberately alienates himself from everyone except her. It's probably the reason the rest of her family have never bonded with him. The mysterious side to him could be the reason why they never made their courting official. It's always just been something they just did.

After Gurley excuses herself, there is an awkward moment between the two. Finally, Martha Lee begins to make her way to the kitchen table, and as she takes a seat, Mr. Eugene does the same. She speaks first. "I've said what needs to be said, Mr. Jean. I can't say anymore... What's left to say?" Objecting, Mr. Eugene says, "But, I have not been able to say anything. You keep hanging up on me! Ms. Martha,

I..." She interrupts him again, reiterating that she has nothing to say. "Oh, stop with all the formalities, Mr. Jean... as far as I'm concerned, chivalry is dead. I'll be referring to you as merely Eugene from now on... that is, if there is ever a reason to refer to you at all ... anymore."

At this, Mr. Jean drops his head, and this time, softens his voice as he pleads with her, saying, "Now, Ms. Martha... umm, Martha... Lord, that doesn't even sound right." He gathers his thoughts and continues, "Ms. Martha, you are just taking things too serious. We have had a good thing going on for the last—what? Sixteen years or so. Why do you want to go and spoil it now? After all these years..." Martha Lee has a mixture of sarcasm, sadness, and anger in her voice as she cuts him off again, "Spoil it? Me? Because after all these years, I've finally come to know the truth about you. You're a no good, two timing... scoundrel!"

He sighs as he tries to defend himself, "But, you're going to take my wife's word for that?" She snaps back, "So, you're confirming that you do have one! If I only had a gun!" There's another uncomfortable moment between the two as Eugene tries to think of something constructive to say. He finds only simple words to plead with. "Now, Ms. Martha, it's complicated. Why don't you give me a chance to explain? You know there is another side to this story." Martha Lee has decided that she's not going to make this easy for him. She can be pretty obstinate when she needs to be, and as far as she's concerned, this is a 'need to be' case.

She harshly speaks to him, "How? You're married! I've been gallivanting for all these years with a married man. End of story... and end of us... The End!" That being said, she tries to finish the conversation before her emotions get the best of her. She rises to show him out of the door, but he doesn't move, so after another difficult moment for them both, she sits back down. Eugene takes a deep breath before he begins to plead his case with Martha Lee. He begins to stammer, "I've... I've finally got up the nerve to move forward with a ... well, a divorce after all these...these miserable years with her. That's why she contacted you today. And it's because she just doesn't want to lose... the house..."

He begins adjusting himself on the kitchen chair in order to gain his composure and another level of comfort. They are sitting at an awkward distance from one another, and this adds to Eugene's discomfort as he comes clean to Martha Lee.

He begins to scoot his chair closer to her, but she stops him with a look of warning in her eyes. He abandons this effort and begins again. He says, "We haven't lived as a couple for the last twenty or more years. Well, we both live under the same roof, but she has her side and I have mines. Years ago, my lawyer advised me to stay in the house and wait for her to leave to file for divorce. That way, I could keep my house and just buy her out."

He pounds his fist on both knees out of frustration from the very thought of his soon-to-be ex-wife's shenanigans over the years. He continues, "Nothing I've done over these years has moved that cantankerous woman to leave... stubborn is her name! A witch! But, Ms. Martha, lately I've been thinking..." Martha Lee cuts him off with a look of the eyes and a raised finger. She's already made up her mind that she's not going to melt in his arms and make nice in order to ease his pain of being found out. No, there is nothing about her, or for this matter, in her, that would make her pretend that what she's just learned about him is not what she learned about him. No, she's learned a long time ago how to show up for herself. So, she proceeds to shut him down.

In a very matter of fact tone, she says, "I don't want to hear what you've been thinking about lately. I just need to ... I just need to be alone. This is all just too much for me to even digest. I want to just be left alone. Eugene, can you please leave and spare me the pain and embarrassment of having thought that I could be the apple of someone's eye?" He leans forward towards her for an intimate moment, hoping this will change her mind. It doesn't. She turns her face away from him. Without saying a word, he rises and walks to the front door, opens it and turns toward her one last time before saying, "I'll leave for now... but this isn't over." He closes the door behind him, and Gurley comes and stands at her sister's side.

From the look on her face, Gurley has been eavesdropping. There's compassion in her voice as she speaks to Martha Lee, "Oh, hey... the food here yet?" Without moving an inch, Martha Lee answers, "No, but there's one of Nettie's red velvet cakes under that cake dish there on the counter. Can you bring it to me? Don't bother for a plate; just bring a fork with it." Gurley locates the cake and brings it with two forks to the table where Martha Lee is sitting. She takes a seat next to her sister and attempts to comfort her. "You okay?" Martha Lee responds with a bit of resolve in her voice, "Nope, I'm not okay. This here cake will get me through the night just fine."

They both dig into the cake with their forks. With a big smile on her face, Gurley says, "Well sis, I hope this doesn't ruin my appetite for my dinner." Martha suddenly stops what's she's doing, and with a worried look on her face, she says, "Hey, where's Eric and Frankie? The house is unusually quiet. Did they make it home from school?" Gurley puts a smirk on her face as she answers, "No, their dad picked them up from school today. He wanted to have dinner and time with them. They should be home by seven or eight."

Martha Lee breaths out a sigh of relief and inquires again, "And Pop-Pop. Where is he?" Gurley says, "Oh, he's back there letting Animal Kingdom watch him. Installing that smart TV in his room was a smart idea, sis; it's the best adult daycare in the world. He can sit in front of that thing all day. You know, I think his dementia is getting worse. The other day, he called me Bertha and actually smiled at me..." "Yes, I suppose he's missing Mamma like crazy. He never did recover from their divorce, and when you were born—well, he did resent you, so if he smiled at you..." Gurley contorts her face as if she's pouting and they both laugh. "But, you know, sis, I love you and Mamma loved you... probably too much for your own good."

They both savor the good flavor of the cake for a moment, and then Martha proceeds with a much needed conversation with Gurley. She asks, "Well, how did the job interview go today?" Without thinking, Gurley tells on herself, but then catches the mistake, "What job interview? Oh yeah, that one... today... it went... well... it, went." Gurley takes another huge bite of the cake in order to dodge the conversation. She mumbles something inaudible as she chews. Martha Lee can't be fooled; she continues to press the issue of work.

She says, "You know that offer still stands. Why don't you let me help you get a job at the school? I know the superintendent, the principal, several teachers..." Gurley continues to fill her mouth with cake as she answers her sister, "No, sis. I need to do this on my own. God blesses the child that's got her own..." Martha Lee raises her eyebrows as she quickly corrects Gurley, "Now, you know that's not scripture, right?!" Still chewing cake, she snaps back, "Yes, it's in the Bible; my Bible. It's in the book of Gurley, chapter forty, verse one!" They both get a good laugh as they continue to devour the cake with their forks.

As Martha's heaviness begins to lighten up, she continues saying to her sister what needs to be said to her. She gently places her fork on the table and very deliberately places both elbows on the table. She then folds her hands and continues. With a serious tone, she says "But, the thing is little sis, you don't have your own and that's what I'm concerned about. It seems to me that you need a little help. It's been almost a good year now since you came to stay for a few months while you 'get yourself together'. Now, I'm not rushing you out, but I just don't want you to stay in this rut ..."

Gurley immediately takes offense. She raises her voice a little, all the while still maintaining a level of respect for the hand that's feeding her, "A rut? I'm not in a rut... I'm just taking my time. I've got to do it right, you know—get back on my feet the right way. I've got to be selective in these jobs... holding out for that right one... you know, once I get out there again, there's no going back, you know... I just need a little more time. The right job will come along; I can feel it..." Martha Lee is not willing to argue with her sister, so she graciously pulls back the pressure and begins to close the subject.

She says to her, "Well, I hope so. It's nice having you and the boys around and all, but I do worry if I'm doing the right thing by you. I don't want to be your enabler..." Gurley quickly agrees, "Oh, it's the right thing. Trust me, it's the right thing. I don't know what we would have done without you, sis. You know I'm grateful, right?" Martha Lee picks up her fork, and before diving into the cake again, she says, "I know what I'm grateful for..." Gurley asks with enthusiasm, "What is that, sis?" As she readies her mouth for a nice chunk of cake, Martha Lee says, "This here cake! Mamma Nettie sure knows how to put her foot in a cake. I'm going to have to order another one, because I'm going through! I'm going to need me some good cake while I'm going through..." Gurley picks up Martha's phone and hands it to her as she speaks, "Yes, girl... thou shalt order another cake... cause I'm going through too!" They both continue to gouge the cake with their forks as Martha makes that call. A few moments later, someone finally picks up on the other end. Martha Lee speaks into the phone, "Hello, Nettie? How are you doing this evening? This cake is good, girl. No, I have the red velvet. Well, since you mentioned it, why don't I give that 7-up cake a try too." As she listens to the response from the other end, she gives her sister a playful wink of the eye.

She responds, "Wow, that quick? Matter of fact, I can have her wig finished by then if she doesn't mind coming to the house to get it installed. Okay, fine. Let Savannah know she can come around ten o'clock in the morning. Alright, it's a date with the cake... Okay, bye-bye now." She hangs up, and they continue to eat the cake and chat. Gurley says, almost singing, "It's a date with the cake..." Martha Lee chimes in saying the same thing, and it becomes a song that they both sing, "It's a date with the cake." The two sisters laugh and giggle like teenagers.

# Chapter Four

## Secrets Uncovered

It's Friday morning and Wendy has managed to keep her suspension from school a secret to the household occupants except for Pop-Pop. Over the past few days, Pop-Pop has eerily made enough quotes to convince her that he knows, but for whatever reason, Wendy knows her secret is safe with him. But, it surely was not easy escaping the feelings of guilt with him lurking about. Nevertheless, she's managed to help the boys each morning with getting out of the house on time for school and not come under scrutiny as to why she's not as competitive for the bathroom each morning or why her signature style makeup is not on.

Earlier, she dropped the boys off at their bus stop as usual, but instead of heading over to the library to spend her day, as she has done during her suspension, she had to make a U-turn because she left her cell phone at home. Instead of making a bee-line out of the house after locating her phone, she lingers in the kitchen trying to make a call to the college again.

Wendy hears someone on the other end pick up and immediately begins her well-practiced speech. Rather hurriedly in a hushed tone, she says, "Hello yes, I'm Wendy Brown. Student #337990—all capitals—WMB. I've been trying to talk with someone about my status—well my scholarship status. I'm wanting to register for early enrollment, but from what I've been told, I don't have a scholarship, even though I do. I have a letter to prove it and... could you check to see if my status has changed? The last four digits ..." Before Wendy has an opportunity to give the rest of her info, she sees her mother coming down the hall. The frustration on Wendy's face could kill someone. She quickly hides her phone after saying, "Okay, can you hold for one moment, please?" She reluctantly places the call on hold in order to greet her mother.

With a surprised look on her face, Martha speaks to her daughter. "Wendy, what are you doing home this late in the morning? You feeling okay?" Martha Lee's hand suddenly lands flush on Wendy's forehead. Trying to hide her frustration, Wendy responds, "Morning, Mom. I'm feeling okay. I'm home ..." She lets her last word linger in the air because Wendy knows that if she says anything else, it would be a lie. Martha Lee gives her a puzzled look as she continues to speak to her daughter, "I know you're home. Okay. Well, you better get off to school. You know how I feel about you taking off from school. Get to school. Hurry along now. Oh, and hand me that bottle of water there on the counter, please." Wendy looks over her shoulder and sees the water. She quickly grabs it and shoves it into her mother's outstretched hand. Martha Lee thanks her and heads back to her bedroom.

When the coast is clear, she returns to her phone call, "Hello, hello... Oh, man... not today, Lord. Help me today, please..." Exasperated, she picks up her keys and handbag before redialing the number to the college. With her phone to her ear, she hurriedly opens the door and comes face-to-face with Savannah Lawson. Savannah is carefully holding a white cardboard box with one hand and was about ready to ring the doorbell with the other. Wendy almost plows Savannah down with her frenzied momentum. Savannah is surprised, "Oh, goodness, Wendy. Good morning. What are you doing home? Are you sick? Where are you going in such a hurry?" Wendy abruptly stops and respectfully greats her, "Oh, hello, Ms. Savannah ...."

She then throws her voice to the back of the house to ensure that her mother hears her, "Mamma... Ms. Savannah is here." She then reassures Savannah as she continues out the door, "Just make yourself at home; she'll be out in a minute. Have a good day." Savannah responds to Wendy as she watches her make haste down the driveway and jump in her car. Savannah says, "Alright, but slow down. Wherever you're going, you want to arrive there safely. Slow down, please. Don't drive like how you running..." Savannah shuts the door and makes her way to the kitchen before placing the white box on the counter.

She continues her thoughts out loud, as Martha Lee joins her in the kitchen. "I'm telling you, these kids today are in such a hurry... it seems like the whole world is in a hurry these days... but people need to slow down ..." Martha Lee greets her, "Well, hello there. What's that you talking about?" Savannah blows it off, "Oh, hey Martha. Nothing really. Now, I put the cake there on the counter. Mamma Nettie wanted me to tell you it's nice and it came fresh out of the oven first thing this morning as promised. What are you celebrating that you have to have so many cakes in such a short time?" Martha's eyes get a little larger than normal as she responds, "Oh, girl. Nothing I'm celebrating; it's what I'm going through... but I don't want to talk about it..." She throws both hands up as Savannah responds, "Well okay, I hope you enjoy the cake."

She turns the conversation to her desired hairstyle. "Now, I was thinking about having you give me a good wash and then an install..." Martha Lee abruptly cuts Savannah off again with a bit of distress in her voice, "It's Mr. Jean! That man done gone and mademe mad. Have some coffee with me." Martha Lee goes to the kitchen counter, grabs two mugs, pours coffee in each of the cups and returns to the kitchen table where they both have a seat. Savannah speaks with a little hesitation, "Well, alright. I guess we can... You suppose we can enjoy one cup of coffee and you can go ahead and finish? I have to be across town ..."

Martha Lee cuts her off and just dives into a full-on dissertation, "I was fooled, and now I look like a fool... bamboozled, hoodwinked, conned, and deceived... duped! How could I have been so blind?! I didn't see this coming... I'm ... I'm undone..." With a look of confusion, Savannah responds, "What on earth are you talking about? Martha Lee, what could be so awful?" Martha is speaking in an uncharacteristically high pitched voice as she continues to complain to Savannah, "It's beyond awful... It's inconceivable,

87

mind-blowing, astounding... quite frankly, I'm, I'm dumbfounded..." Savannah says, "Okay, what has happened that you are so expressive this morning?" Martha Lee continues in the same high pitched tone, "He's married... Mr. Jean is married..."

Savannah very casually responds, "What?! Married?! That don't even sound right... married? Mr. Jean? Why, we were all just out together the other night... ... When did he get married?" Martha Lee continues in her regular voice, "But, why am I surprised? All these years... all these years of ... nothing, really." Savannah is confused, "But, when did he get married and to who?!" Martha Lee continues to whine, "He's been married for sometime... oh, about twenty years to be exact... his wife called me on yesterday... she had plenty to say. Savannah, the woman sound so ugly, belligerent ..."

Savannah is still confused and is not able to digest this information as fast as she's hearing it. She says, "But wait, you lost me on twenty years. You're telling me that... that impeccably mannered gentlemen who is so, ... so noble... is NOT so noble, but is a con man? He's been conning you... us?! Are you sure? This is mind-blowing! It's inconceivable, astounding... quite frankly, I'm dumbfounded..." Savannah takes a moment to gather her thoughts while Martha Lee stares at her in dismay. After a moment, Savannah continues with a glimmer of hope, "Are you sure? How do you know you were actually talking to his wife? It could have been some woman playing games... or maybe, he's been separated and she was long gone and just popped up..."

Martha Lee answers with finality in her voice, "Because he confirmed it! Along with an explanation... He's just 'sharing the same roof with her' ... but as far as I'm concerned, explanation or not ... how can I believe anything he has to say or, better yet, nothing he has to say matters at this point... He's married!" Martha Lee changes her tone from wrath to regret as they continue to sip their coffee. She says, "Sixteen years, Savannah ... almost! I've spent these years of my life with a man... I feel like I don't know him. What does that say about me? How could I have not known all these years?"

Martha Lee looks at her stunned friend, and then answers her own rhetorical question. She does this as she takes Savannah's coffee cup from her just as it reaches her lips for the last sip. "No words ... I know! Come on, we had better get you started before the time gets away from us..." Martha Lee walks over to the kitchen sink, drops the cups down in it, and they both make their way across the living room and down the hall to Martha Lee's in-home hair studio.

Moments later, Gurley, still dressed in her sleepwear, enters the kitchen just as her cell phone rings. She answers in a curt tone, "Jelloooo! Yes, this is she. Whom may I ask is calling this early in the morning?" As Gurley answers her phone, Wendy peaks her head into the front door, and then sneakily tries to move past Gurley who has her back turned. "Yes, I did submit a resume a few weeks ago. Yes, I know I'm very qualified. I have a degree. Well, what time will the interview be? Ten o'clock AM in the morning? No, that's a little too early for me. What are the hours of the job? Nine to five PM? Hey, when I put the application in, I was interested. I'm no longer interested. Thank you."

Gurley hangs up and proceeds to the fridge as Wendy begins to talk to her. Gurley is a little startled at the sound of Wendy's voice, "Did I just hear right?! Did you just turn down a job? Is that what you've been doing all this time? How do you have the nerve to lay around this house ..." Gurley cuts Wendy off using her signature curtness, "Mind your own business, little girl. Matter of fact, stay out of grown folk business ..."

Appalled at Gurley's demand for respect, Wendy snaps back at her, "What grown person do you see around here? I know how to mind my manners... if there was a grown person standing in front of me, I would stay out of their business... how could you be grown when you insist my Mamma is your Mamma?"

Gurley yells, "Hey, you better watch your mouth and tone with me, Wendy..." Raising the volume of her voice to match Gurley's, Wendy continues her train of thought, "... and every chance you get, you're taking money from her and eating her out of house and home..." They are now in a full blown screaming match when Gurley screams, "I'm warning you to shut up, Wendy. It's too early for this!" But, Wendy doesn't let up. "Let me remind you that I let you stay in my bedroom almost a year ago... on a promise that it would just be for a few months, till you get yourself together." Defensive, Gurley shouts at Wendy, "You want your room back? Well then, take it. You're an Indian giver!"

Wendy is flabbergasted and takes on a sarcastic tone, mocking her aunt as she throws her hands in the air, "Indian giver?! How childish! Grown folk, huh?!" Wendy, then loses her self-control and blurts out at the top of her lungs to Gurley, "I don't want my room back. I want you to grow up, get a job and leave.... I'm a teenager and I work harder than you do... and stop taking advantage of my Mamma, your sister!" Gurley responds to Wendy as if she didn't hear Wendy's last objections, "And why aren't you in school today?" Wendy responds with the same intensity, "Stay out of grown folk business..." At this, Martha Lee and Savannah, whose hair is wrapped in a towel, come hurriedly into the room as if some sudden tragic accident has occurred.

Martha attempts to bring order. "Hey, hey, hey... what's going on in here? I know that's not you two talking like that to one another. You both sound like two strangers in a street fight!" In the next few moments, order is restored. Afterwards, Martha Lee begins to speak in a calm and quiet tone. Looking at Wendy, but talking to both of them, she begins to correct them, "We don't talk like this to one another... and you know this. What's going on in here?" Wendy has regained her respectful, teenage composure to some degree as she answers her mother, "Nothing... Not a thing... Just your sister is all..."
Still glaring at her daughter, Martha Lee pleads with her, "Wendy, sweetheart, what has gotten into you?" Wendy has almost shaken off the vexation caused by the moments before when Gurley instigates her

again, "You better tell her, Mamma..." Wendy loses it again and shouts at Gurley from the top of her lungs, "She's not your Mamma!"

Martha Lee and Savannah yell at the same time, "Wendy!" It isn't because of what she has said, but they are both surprised and appalled at Wendy's rude outburst. Martha Lee has gotten a little anxious at this point as she tries to navigate her thoughts through the moment. She proceeds to try to make sense out of everything, "Wendy, this is not you. This is not my daughter... and why aren't you in school? Did you even go today? What is going on? I need an answer right this moment..." Gurley, who has not learned the value of keeping her mouth closed for the sake of peace, blurts out, "That's what I was trying to understand... she is off ...?" Martha Lee quickly rebukes her, "Hush, Gurley!" Before Martha Lee could finish hushing her sister, Wendy blurts out her secret, "I got suspended from school on Monday. Principal McClain suspended me until Monday."

At this, Savannah quietly excuses herself in the direction of the hair studio. Martha Lee has to ask Gurley to leave. With a bit of irritation, she says, "Gurley, can you give me a moment with my daughter, please? Maybe you should jump in the shower in order to start your productive day of job hunting..." Obviously offended and a little embarrassed, Gurley leaves. Martha beckons her daughter to the living room couch for a calm talk. Wendy complies, and with every step she takes toward her mom, she shakes off the aggression from the moments before. By the time she takes a seat next to her mom, Wendy appears to be her old, laid back self.

Martha Lee begins, "Before you say anything, I want you to know that I trust you. I know that there is an honest to goodness reason for these... your... shenanigans! But what have you been doing all week? Here it is, Friday... you were suspended on Monday. Why?" Her voice trails off as she begins to scratch her head because she is at a loss for words. Wendy proceeds to explain in a calm apologetic manner, "I spent a lot of time at the library this week. I just didn't want to bother you. You seemed to be in another place lately. But Ma, I really don't know what's going on... I don't have an explanation as to why I was suspended. Principal McClain said it was because..." Out of frustration, she stops mid sentence, takes a breath, and continues using a different tone; it was more like a 'coming clean' manner of speech. She says, "I think it was because I didn't break up a fight in the girls' bathroom..." At this, Martha Lee is taken aback, "You didn't?! Was it because they had guns and knives and the girls were giants?" They each share a warm chuckle that seems to lighten the mood. Then Wendy answers her mom, "Well, I did break it up... eventually, but I sure as heck didn't want to..." Again, Martha Lee answers with a tinge of surprise, "You didn't?"

Wendy begins to plead with her mom, "No! Ma, you just don't understand. The kids at my school, I don't relate and I don't want to. It seems to me like that would be just too much work. They got issues... problems! Half of them on drugs, the other half got parent issues, boyfriend drama... girlfriend drama... it's crazy! They act like they don't even care about their lives. So, why should I care? Besides, these teens today act like they have alien hormones... they do some crazy stuff that no man could dream of. I just want to escape school and get on to college. This is what happens; you start getting involved and you end up where I sit today... suspended..."

Martha Lee marvels at what she's just learned about her daughter, "You're a senior in high school and I never knew this about you." Wendy quickly responds to her mom, "Well let's not make such a big deal about it... Mom, we are just talking and I'm just, well, I'm just saying... that's that. I'll be back to school on Monday and this will all be behind me. I just have to find a way to stay out of Principal McClain's way. Lately, she's after me to join some group at school... she says it will be better for me in college if I showed some interest in people..."

Martha Lee chuckles, "Well, Wendy, is that such a bad idea?" Wendy, wishing to shut down any hope that her mother might have of her otherwise, says, "Mom, not interested. People are too much work. Just look at your sister; case in point. You start getting involved and people start adopting you as family. I can't imagine girls following me around at school telling me they owe me their life for what I did... besides, I have nothing to offer anyone ..." In a more serious tone, Martha Lee retorts, "Perhaps, you could do some good. When you were a child, I used to call you wise ole soul because you just had wisdom beyond your years. Lord, you came out the womb..."

Before she gets too mushy, Wendy cuts her mom off mid-sentence, "Ma, I already did some good... I completed my community service requirements and was involved in school activities in order to complete my college applications. I'm accepted, with full scholarship. What more do I need to give... all of me?!" They both laugh at this last statement. Afterwards, Martha Lee takes a deep breath, exhales and then looks at her daughter with resolve and relief before breaking the silence again. "Well, do I need to put in a call to my friend Jean McClain and tell her to leave my baby alone? ..." Wendy waves her hand at her mom rejecting this idea, "No, Mom. I'm good. I'm good..." There's another moment of silence wherein Martha Lee becomes overwhelmed by the sudden emotions of pride and joy as she thinks about how independent her daughter is.

After a moment, Martha Lee takes on a more serious tone as she changes the subject. She gently speaks to her daughter, "You good with this living situation?! Now, I know having Gurley and the boys here puts a little strain on things... I can talk to her about giving your room back if that would help. You were so gracious to volunteer it..." Wendy interjects, "No, I'm good, Mom... besides... have you taken a look at that room? Can you imagine if they were bunking out here in our living space?"

Martha takes a quick look around the tidy living room. While so doing, she imagines what it would look like if her house guest took over the living room. Apparently, she doesn't like what she's imagined, "Ooooh ... You have a point, but are you sure about this? I know teens need their private space too..." Reassuring her mother, Wendy says to her, "Yeah, that's the case; we do, but I'm no ordinary teen, right?!" The doorbell rings, and as Martha rises to answer the door, she says, "Yeah, that's the truth... wise ole soul." They both laugh as she opens the door to Vera Wells, a rather plain young woman in her late twenties.

Martha Lee is a bit startled as she tries to recall how she knows the familiar face. Then, she remembers the recent encounter at the local market. Martha Lee came to her rescue, giving her the balance due for her grocery total. The young woman then struck up a friendly conversation with her. She quickly greets her, "Oh, hello... it's Vera, right? Come on in. What can I do for you?" As Vera steps into the house, Martha Lee notices the young woman's disheveled clothes and how tired she looks. She has a fleeting thought that the woman looks much too young to look so tired. She brushes it off as Vera speaks to her, "Oh, I was just stopping by to confirm dinner tonight..."

From where she's sitting on the couch, Wendy suddenly gasps upon hearing Vera's words, and Martha Lee quickly covers up Wendy's rude outburst with her response, "Oh yes, of course... wait that's tonight?" Vera timidly says, "Ummm, it doesn't have to be. We can..." Martha Lee quickly stops her, "Oh, nonsense! Of course, dinner tonight. About seven o'clock would be perfect... bring your three kids and we will have a good ole time getting acquainted. We'll order some pizza and keep it simple if you don't' mind ..."

Martha Lee turns her attention to Wendy, "Oh, Wendy, you haven't met our new neighbors, have you? This is Ms. Vera Wells. Say hello." Very pleasantly, Wendy says, "Hello and welcome to the neighborhood." Continuing to speak to her daughter, she says, "Ms. Vera has three children. Now, I understand the oldest is in high school? Wendy, have you met her daughter?" Wendy quickly shoots down the idea of having made friends with any new kids, "I doubt it. I don't be paying attention to who comes and who goes..."

Wendy's phrasing comes off a little too rude for Martha Lee's good manners, so she awkwardly tries to cover up her daughter's remarks. "Umm, she means, she's just so busy getting good grades to notice... anyway, we'll meet the kids tonight... see you at seven o'clock, okay?" Vera responds with a pleasant smile, "Yes, thanks for having us. Seven, it is." Vera turns to Wendy, and before leaving says, "Well, nice to meet you, Wendy. We will see you later." She leaves, and as Martha Lee closes the door behind her, Wendy begins to whine, "Mom, really?! Why do you have to be the welcome committee? I don't wanna meet nobody ... who goes to my school... who lives next door..." Martha Lee chuckles to herself as she consoles Wendy. "Well, they live down the street... You'll be just fine... oh, I forgot about Savannah." Martha Lee makes a beeline to the back of the house where Savannah has been waiting, leaving Wendy alone in the living room.

After a moment of thinking to herself, Wendy picks up her cell phone and begins to dial the university again. Almost immediately, she hears a busy signal. Frustrated, she tosses the phone aside and exclaims out loud, "Uuuuugggghhh, why does everything have to be so difficult?!" She throws her head down between her hands on her lap. After a moment, she looks up towards the sky and speaks to God, "Dear God, I'm only a teenager..."

Immediately she hears a voice respond back to her, "Everything will be okay in the end. If it's not okay, then it's not the end." Startled and frightened, Wendy quickly looks around the room, expecting to find God, Himself. Instead, she gets a glimpse of Pop-Pop before he disappears into the bathroom. He says, "John Lennon said that." With those words, he closes the door. Wendy sits relaxed on the couch marveling at how her senile Pop-Pop always shows up with the most perfect thing to say at the most perfect time.

Hours later, Wendy, Frankie and Eric are doing their homework in the living room. They have their school books, book bags, computers and other devices sprawled out over the spacious room. Eric, whose doing more horse playing than homework, is in the middle of the living room floor standing on his head with his legs dangling above him. He's shouting out knock-knock jokes as Wendy, half listening, coaxes him back to doing his homework.

She very patiently says, "Come on, Spider Man. It's time to do homework. Here's a riddle for you—if Batman had five bags of ten marbles, and he gave six marbles to Robin, how many marbles does he have?" Eric, still standing on his head, says, "Knock, knock." Wendy reluctantly responds, "Who's there?" Eric answers in a playful tone, "Forty-four marbles knocking on the door." Just then, the doorbell rings. Wendy throws her voice to the back of the house to alert her mother. "Mom, your company is here, or it's the pizza!" She begins to instruct the boys to help her gather up their belongings as Martha Lee scurries to the door.

It's the pizza delivery guy with a small stack of pizza boxes accompanied by a few large bags. Shortly after, Gurley comes through the open door with several shopping bags in tow. She quickly tries to make her way to the bedroom. Martha Lee makes the exchange with the pizza guy by handing her bank card over to him, "Add yourself a tip," she says to him. Wendy gets a glimpse of Gurley's designer shopping bags. As they lock eyes with one another, Gurley tries to divert the attention away from her shopping indulgence to the pizza. While making her way across the living room, she says, "Just what I was having a taste for tonight. Did you order me some of those chicken wings? I'll be right back."

Wendy steps in Gurley's pathway and begins to inspect the bags that she's trying to hide. She says, "Wait, what?! Are you still getting an unemployment check? What did you get at the Gucci Store that you can afford, Aunt Gurley?!" Angry, but not willing to make a scene, she nervously responds, "Mind your own business, Wendy!" She tries to walk around

Wendy, but Wendy blocks her every move. Annoyed, Gurley cries for help, "Mamma, tell her..." Wendy blatantly cuts her off before she can finish, "Tell me what, Gurley? What is your SISTER going to tell me? To stop noticing all those designer shopping bags you have in your hand?" Martha Lee, wishing to keep the peace, steps in, "You two, don't start!" Wendy relents as Gurley proceeds down the hall en route to her living quarters.

Martha Lee looks at the receipt the pizza delivery guy just texted her cell phone and is flabbergasted. "I said a tip, not a mortgage payment!" The delivery guy scratches his head as he responds, "Oh, I'm just out here tryin' to make a living, you know..." Martha Lee answers, "A living?! Boy, bye. He leaves as Vera and her three children arrive and Gurley comes back into the living room quietly greeting her boys. Turning her attention to her newly arrived guests, Martha Lee greets them with an energetic smile, "Oh, y'all are just in time. Come on in; the pizza just arrived."

Wendy looks up and immediately recognizes Mae, the schoolmate whom she rescued earlier in the week. She is paralyzed as she locks eyes with her. Vera responds to Martha's warm greeting with the same level of energy, "Oh, that's great. Thank you so much for having us tonight. This is my baby, April, my eldest, Mae, and, my son Junie ..." Gurley interjects with a smirk and a laugh, "Excuse me, ma'am, but..." She begins to exaggerate, looking over her shoulders to her left and then right side, and finally, underneath the dining table as if she's looking for something.

Martha Lee inquires, "Gurley girl, what are you doing? What are you looking for?" Laughing at her own wit, Gurley answers, "Oh, I'm just looking for July! ... April, Mae, June... July... get it?" Martha Lee ignores the joke and proceeds to introduce her family, but Junie interrupts her. He says with sad puppy-like eyes, "Ma'am, July died..." There is a moment of sympathetic silence until Vera interrupts it. She angrily reprimands her son, "Junie! What have I told you about that lying, boy?!"

After a quick moment of relief, Gurley responds to Junie, "Oh, you got jokes, huh?" Junie sassily snaps back at her "That's what you get for trying to make a joke..." He cuts a few of the latest dance moves to taunt her. Vera attempts to shut him down, "Will you calm down, Junie?! Go over there and sit your butt down ... Now! I bet' not hear one word outta you!" Junie uses the same dance moves to make his way over to Eric and Frankie.

When he reaches them, the two join in with their own dance moves, but Wendy quickly calms them all down and steers them to their PlayStation. Gurley speaks out to anyone who is listening, "Oh, that's a spunky one right there..." Ignoring Gurley, Martha Lee is determined to get through the awkward moment, "Ms. Vera, this is my sister, Gurley, and my daughter, Wendy, but you have already met her... but Mae, now, have you met Wendy?" There is an awkward silence and neither Wendy nor Mae will be the first to speak up.

Mae finally breaks the ice. "Yes, she's the one who rescued me from those girls on Monday." Mae turns to Wendy and speaks directly to her, "I didn't get a chance to thank you. I owe you one." Wendy uncomfortably brushes off the peace offering from Mae. She shrugs her shoulders and takes a step backwards as she speaks, "Ah, yeah. No, we're good..." But catching on, Martha Lee steps in, "Is this about that thing?" Wendy continues to attempt to brush the topic off, "Yeah, Mom. Can we just get to eating the pizza?" Vera adds momentum to the topic as she inquires to Wendy, "But, I wish someone would make me understand what happened. I can't trust this one with the truth... two weeks in a new school and she's already suspended."

She turns to her daughter and says, "How does trouble find you that quick?" With a little disrespect in her voice, Mae responds to her mother, "I've already told you that it wasn't my fault! What?! You wanted me to stand there and take a beat down?! Here's my witness... Wendy, could you please tell my mom that it wasn't my fault?!" Wendy flashes a quick glance at Martha Lee, possibly for help, and then begins to stutter, "Well, I really don't ... ummm. I don't want to get involved... I ummm, I didn't see the whole thing... but um..." Vera interjects, "You're the one that took up for Mae, right? But, from what I understand, you were suspended as well, right? Pardon me, please ... If you don't know, then how were you also suspended?"

Wendy raises her hands, and exacerbated, she responds, hoping to put an end to the conversation, "At the wrong time, I was in the wrong place! It's a misfortune for me since I was on the outside looking in ... see, I should not have been looking at all, then I would not have broken up a fight and rescued you from being bullied... and subsequently, got suspended ... for doing a good deed..." Excitedly, Mae cuts her off, pointing out the proof of truth to her mom, "See, Mom! I told you... I was being bullied! Now, do you believe me?" Martha Lee gets a look at Wendy's countenance and remembers their earlier conversation. She decides to bail her daughter out of the conversation. "You know, enough of this school talk... this pizza is getting cold. Let's sit down and dig in. Gurley, give me a hand, will you?" Along with Ms. Vera, they both begin to open the boxes and serve the family.

Mae approaches Wendy at the couch where she is sitting alone nibbling on her pizza.
After a moment, Mae speaks. "Thanks for having my back for a minute there. I thought you were going to leave me hanging..." Wendy curtly cuts her off, "It's behind us now. Monday we'll be back in school ... so everything is cool..." Mae takes a bite of her pizza and begins to talk and chew, attempting to make small talk with Wendy, "So, what's your deal?" Wendy gives her a sour look, but Mae is undeterred, "I mean, I don't know... like what type of things you like to do? You like to read, play games... go to the theater... I'm just asking since you're my new best friend... I mean, I should know a little something about you other than where you live..." Wendy horridly objects, "New best... ummm wait. No, that's not accurate..."

Just then, the doorbell rings and Wendy jumps up to answer it. She hopes to rescue herself from Mae, but Mae follows her to the door. Wendy opens the door to an inquisitive Amber. There is an awkward moment between the three as Amber makes her way inside the house and begins to take a quick assessment of the 'party'. "Oh", she says, "I was just dropping by to check on you and to keep you company. Didn't know I'd be intruding on a party..." Wendy casually responds, "It's not a party; you're not intruding... come on in..." Wendy takes Amber by the hand and leads her back to the living room couch as if Amber was a prized jewel. Mae follows close behind.

Before they take their seats, Wendy gives Mae a formal introduction to Amber, "This is my best friend, Amber. Amber, meet Mae..." Mae gives Amber a warm smile and says, "Well, if you're my new best friend's friend, then you're my new second best friend ..." She offers her hand to Amber. When Amber takes too long to comply, Mae goes in for an awkward hug. After their greetings, they each take a space on the couch. Mae wrestles with an oblivious Amber to sit closest to Wendy. Afterwards, Mae speaks to them both, "Do either of you have boyfriends? If not, I know how to hook you up." Just then, the doorbell rings.

Martha Lee has been in the kitchen with Vera and Gurley as they dote over April and make small talk about little girls. As she excuses herself to answer the door, she takes a quick glance around her home. She sees Frankie and Eric having fun on their PlayStation with their new friend, Junie. Pop-Pop is sitting in his reclining chair, calmly watching the boys' PlayStation game as if it's the latest blockbuster film. She sees the three girls awkwardly sitting together in the living room, and she can't help but to feel a sense of wholesome warmth and serenity as she moves closer to the door.

Mr. Jean stands in front of her with a bouquet of flowers. Her tranquility is short-lived as Mr. Jean begins to plead, "I ..." She quickly cuts him off, "I told you, I'm not interested..." She discretely closes the door without having taken the flowers. After a moment to herself, Martha Lee rejoins the conversation in the kitchen without drawing any attention to the awkward situation she's just encountered. After another moment, she excuses herself to cut a large piece of cake and begins to eat it standing alone at the opposite end of her kitchen. Junie comes and stands in front of Martha Lee. He speaks when he has her attention, "Ms. Martha, if there is any pizza left over, can we take it with us since we don't' have anything to eat, ... ummm, where we live? I like pizza for breakfast..."

Martha Lee puts the half-eaten piece of cake on the counter and answers him, "Sure, Junie, sure... You know..., I have an idea." She gets everyone's attention, then makes her announcement, "You know, since everyone is having such a good time tonight, why don't we do this right?! I'll cook a good home-cooked meal. Vera, we would love it if you and the kids would be our guest again tomorrow night." She glances at Wendy, "Right, Wendy?!" Wendy's words seem to be stuck in her throat as she chokes for a moment. But, Junie relieves the moment with his excitement, "Okay, cool. Can you like, fry some chicken and make some mac and cheese ... with a lot of cheese? I like a lot of cheese... and... I like ice tea or lemonade, and can we have cake?"

Some laughs and inaudible playful words can be heard, but Vera is horrified. She says, "Junie! ... that's rude... I told you not to embarrass me, didn't I?! Get over here, boy!" He begins to whine, "What?! I'm just ... we haven't... What did I do?" Gurley speaks to whoever can hear, "I told you, this one is off the chain..." Vera turns her attention to Martha Lee, "Umm, are you sure? Ms. Martha, we don't want to impose on you and your family..." But Martha Lee quickly responds, "Nonsense, it will be our pleasure. I can even give you a fresh hair-do tomorrow. It will be

sort of my welcome to the neighborhood gift to you."
The ladies then begin a conversation about hair.
Junie helps himself to a big piece of cake, and then
resumes his spot for next at the PlayStation.

The girls are left in awkwardness. Mae does most of
the talking; it could be that it's her way of dealing with
nervousness. However, outwardly, she seems to be a
pretty confident girl. She rambles as Wendy and
Amber sit bewildered, each with a look of fright on
their faces, "Oh, wow. I see us moving quickly from
friendship to family! So Amber, what's your story? I
mean, what do you like to do... movies, concerts...
boys? Now, me? I like boys! Tell me again, do either
of you have boyfriends? I can hook you up. It's really
not as difficult as you would think to get one... I mean,
it's been only two weeks and I already like did, how
many?"

She stops talking long enough to count in her head,
then resumes, "Oh, I don't know... Wendy, girl. That's
why Doris was so mad... rumor out... there's a new
some 'body' in town." She abruptly stops mid-
sentence, stands to her feet and looks Wendy up and
down. After a brief moment, she speaks again, "Hold
up. Stand up and turn around for me. I just want to
see what we working with..." Now, this is where

Wendy draws the line. She says very casually, "Not happening..." Mae lets out a kind of 'party animal' whine, "What?! We need to turn up!" Both Wendy and Amber are flabbergasted. Mae plops down on the couch near them and begins to make her case on how to get a boyfriend to them.

# Chapter Five

## Dysfunction at its Finest

Wendy is asleep on the couch. The house is still and dark. She is startled awake by an unknown presence. As she opens her eyes, she sees a slow moving dark shadow lurking about. Wendy jumps to her feet, holding a shoe up as if it were a dangerous weapon. With her heart racing, she speaks through the darkness, "What the what...?! Who's that?!" After a scary moment, Gurley speaks up. "Girl, go back to sleep... it's just me!" Gurley trips over something as she tries to sneak past her niece. Staggering, she is obviously drunk, and she smells like club smoke and strong drinks. With her heart beginning to slow its pace, Wendy scolds her aunt, "You're going to do this one too many nights, Gurley." She tosses the shoe to the floor as she gets a whiff of the odor Gurley has carried with her from wherever she's been. "Ooooh, my gosh! What?! Did you bring the whole bar home with you?! You smell like it... please stop breathing, Gurley. You're going to make me drunk."

Slurring as bad as she's walking, Gurley replies, "Shhhh, you're going to wake up the whole house." Wendy retorts, "No, you're going to do that all on your own. Good luck getting to the bedroom without falling flat on your face." Gurley begins to plead with her niece, "I know. Come be a good niece and help me to the door." Wendy complies and comes to help her as Gurley continues to whine with a slurred speech pattern, "You're such a good niece... I know my little dirty secret is safe with you ... it's just between you and me... you got my back." Wendy speaks up to correct her aunt's thinking, "Actually Gurley, I got my Mamma's back... I'm trying to stay out of the way for you to step up and do the right thing. You need to come clean...don't think for one minute that I'm alright with this." They disappear into the bedroom.

After a few moments, Wendy comes back to the living room. No sooner than she returns does Martha Lee appear fully dressed with lots of energy. Upon seeing Wendy, she says, "Oh, good. You're up... I was hoping not to disturb you this early. What are you doing up this early? Is that cigarette smoke? What is that... it smells weird in here? Not willing to get into a long conversation with her mom so early, she slips back into her sleeping position as she answers her, "I ... I'm not quite awake... it's still early, isn't it?

Where are you going this early?" Martha Lee energetically responds, "Well, I wanted to run to the meat market, get some things for the dinner tonight... you know, beat the Saturday traffic and crowd. Get back in time to do Vera's hair today. She could use a good wash, cut and style, you know..."

Annoyed, Wendy responds as she wrestles with her blanket, "Yeah, but Mom... do you have to be so extra?!" Martha is dumbfounded, "Extra?" Wendy explains, "Yeah, dinner tonight, again... with the new neighbors... volunteering to give a free hairdo... Why do you have to invite them into such close proximity to us so soon? They just moved here... we don't even know them ... they could be crazy." Martha Lee stands still for a moment to emphasize the importance of what she's getting ready to say. She can hear compassion in her mother's voice as she speaks, "Wendy, did you get a good look at that boy?! Did you see how he was eating? Good Lord, like he hadn't had a meal all year... and that Mae, she looks like she's troubled..." Wendy is not moved by her mother's compassion, "You mean trouble! She LOOKS LIKE trouble..."

Martha Lee is quick to correct Wendy's lack of compassion. She says, with a sense of sternness,

"Wendy, sometimes people need a helping hand. That family is struggling... something is not right. Now, I know what it's like to be a single mom and young... besides... it will be good to spend time with my favorite girl; that's you. Let's share some laughs tonight as we do something good for someone else for a change." Martha Lee has a moment of nostalgia as she continues, "I haven't cooked a home-cooked meal ... well, in a very long time..." She speaks under her breath for a moment, "Lord knows I could sure use the distraction." She continues her conversation with Wendy, "Besides... it's going to be right-nice to see the look on that boy's face when he sits down to eat everything he requested for dinner... don't you think?"

Wendy doesn't seem to be impressed with the opportunity to 'do good'. She begins to think that there is more to the story and it probably has to do with Mr. Jean not being around lately. She casually approaches the subject with her mother, "Where's Mr. Jean been? You're usually with him on Saturday nights." Martha Lee is quick to respond, "Yes, well, I suppose seasons end." She has a moment in her own thoughts, and then finishes her statement, "Now, don't they?" Not willing to go down this emotional road with her daughter, Martha Lee abruptly ends the discussion before it can get underway, "Well, I'd better get going if I want to beat the Saturday crowds. Please air out this house this morning... it seems a little musty in here..."

Martha Lee picks up her cell phone and begins to dial a number. Wendy makes one last plea with her mother, "Ma, I really don't want to be here tonight... that girl is..." It seems Wendy has lost her mother's attention. "Hello, Mamma Nettie, hold a second, will you?" Martha Lee speaks to Wendy, "Where else you going to be... Amber will be here tonight as well. I invited her..." She throws a kiss to her daughter and resumes her conversation with Mamma Nettie as she exits the front door.

Wendy rolls over, hoping to fall back asleep. Haunted by the prospect of the coming evening's events, she suddenly cries out, "Why God... why me?! I just want to be... alone.... these people!" Just then, she hears Pop-Pop's familiar voice saying, "We must learn to suffer more." He makes his way down the hall, and just before he disappears into the bathroom, he says, "T.S. Elliot said that." Wendy kicks her feet into the air and throws the pillow over her head.

Hours later, Martha Lee and Vera Wells, who is wearing a new hairstyle, are in the kitchen preparing some of the food for the evening's festivities. Martha Lee notices a change in Vera. The new hairstyle seems to have transformed her personality. She seems to be more relaxed, happier and definitely more animated. Vera turns to Martha Lee and says, "I really love my new hairstyle. It's been a while since I've been able to get my hair done." Martha Lee is delighted to hear this, but she plays her generosity down a bit, "Oh, I know about that. Single mother issues. But it's my pleasure." Vera continues, "Well, thank you. And thank you for this—this feast you're preparing... you just don't know what this means to me and my children..."

At this, Martha stops her business for a moment of transparency with Vera. She says, "Vera, I have a little confession... a nice big dinner with my daughter, a house full of people and laughter does my soul good. It's just what the doctor ordered. It's been years since I've done anything remotely close to this. When Wendy was a toddler, I'd have my friends over, a house full just about every weekend. Boy, did we have a good time. I miss those days..." Vera nods her head, and then looks at her watch, "Well, it looks like everything is pretty much done here. I'd better run

and get the kids before Junie starts blowing up my
phone. I should be back in about fifteen or twenty
minutes, at most."

She heads for the door and Martha Lee follows her,
inquiring, "Oh, by the way, which house is it that you
live in?" Vera vaguely answers, "Oh, umm, the ... the
white one... up the street there... and umm, just
around the corner. You know what, I'd better go on
now so I can get back. Okay, see you in a few
minutes." She quickly leaves. Martha Lee continues in
the kitchen preparing for the party and immediately
becomes lost in her thoughts. Gurley comes out of the
bedroom area; her hoarse voice booms through the
silence and startles Martha Lee. "What's going on in
here... you have this house smelling good. Food smell
so good, it woke me up out of a R.E.M sleep! I woke
up drooling..."

Martha gathers her composure as she takes an
assessment of her sister, "Oh, you up and dressed. I
was just thinking whether I should wake you up or
not... it's well into the day! Why are you sleeping so
much lately? Something going on with you that I need
to know about? Gurley backs away from her sister.
She has a sudden case of paranoia, wondering if the
odor from the night before can still be detected oozing

from her person. She tries not to breathe as she talks to her sister. "No, no... why would you think that?" Martha Lee responds rather matter-of-fact like, "Because you've been sleeping all through the day everyday ... Which brings me to my next inquiry... how's the job hunting coming along?"

Gurley gets a little defensive, "It's coming along... but there really isn't anything to talk about... I still have not found a job... is that a problem?" Martha Lee becomes more forceful, "Yes, Gurley, it is a problem. You need to be working, doing something productive... and..." Gurley cuts her off, not willing to hear a lecture. She says, "I'm a grown woman, don't tell me what I need to be doing!" There is silence for a long moment. Martha Lee goes back to preparing her food. Finally, she breaks the silence by casually inquiring about the boys, "Where are the boys? I have not seen them all day." Gurley answers just as casual, "Oh, they are back there cleaning up. Doing more clowning than cleaning though."

Martha Lee makes another attempt at her point to Gurley. She says, "What do you think about the example you are setting to your boys? You know, they do look to you for leadership." Gurley continues in the conversation with her sister with a more respectful tone. She ignores the topic, refusing to take the bait and says, "Now look, I'm not trying to have a bad day today. Don't you have a dinner party to host in a little while? What can I do to help, sis?" Martha looks up from what she is doing and gives her sister a long hard look. She then speaks, "You can begin to set the plates and dinnerware out. We're doing buffet style tonight." Gurley changes her attitude to a more playful one, probably because she's escaped the truthful scrutiny of her sister yet again.

She begins to busy herself with the dishes and dinnerware as Martha Lee says to her, "At some point, you're going to have to deal with the elephant in your room... I believe that time is speedily approaching you. Just remember, when you finally do have to face it, it will be for your good!" Ignoring her sister, Gurley inquires, "Is there any ginger-ale? I could use a cold fizzy drink." The doorbell rings. Martha Lee stops what she's doing and makes her way to the door to answer it. Mr. Jean is on the other side of the door, standing with flowers in one hand. This time, he quickly puts his foot in the door before she has a chance to close it. She speaks to him without a greeting, "Nothing to say. Nothing to talk about, Mr. Jean. Please, move on with your life. I will not change my mind."

Mr. Jean responds, "That's it?! Just like that! Without giving us a chance?!" Martha Lee exclaims, "A chance?! You're married... this case is closed!" Refusing to accept her words, he pleads with her, "I've called you every day. You don't answer your phone. You have not given me an opportunity to fight for us." He stops for a moment, inhales a deep breath, exhales and continues with a softer tone, "I've been fighting for us since I met you, Ms. Martha... but now, I'm ready to ..." Martha Lee curtly responds, cutting him off, "You're ready to what? Come clean? Your WIFE beat you to it!" He continues to plead with her, "We can have a good life together. I can make you happy. We can be happy... at least, let's talk. If this is really the end of us, I need closure." Coldly, Martha Lee says to him, "This is really the end of us and consider this case closed. Goodbye, Eugene."

She asks him to move his foot without saying a word. He complies, and once again, she politely closes the door. She goes back to what she was doing without saying a word or looking at her sister. After a moment, with great satisfaction in her voice, Gurley says, "Yeah, you be knowing about those elephants... huh?!" Just then Wendy and Amber both come through the front door. Amber makes a beeline to the kitchen. She greets Martha Lee with a hug, a kiss and lots of energy, Wendy plops down on a chair that's close by. Amber speaks first, "Hello Ms. Martha, I had a good time last night and I'm ready to do it again... and I'm hungry too!"

Martha Lee regains her composure and greets the two with a carefree attitude. She answers Amber, "Well, hello to you too. I'm glad because we got a lot of food here." She then turns to her beloved daughter and says, "You're too tired to greet your mother with a kiss, daughter? Where y'all been all day?" Without moving, Wendy, simply blows her mother a kiss, and then speaks, "Love you, Mom. We were at Youth Explosion at the church, which I completely forgot about." Noticing that Wendy is leaving out a lot of detail, Amber announces, "Guess who was chosen as youth ambassador for this year? Drum roll, please... Wendy Brown!" With a little sarcasm, Wendy says, "Yeah, Hooray! Hoorah!"

Martha Lee gets a good chuckle in at Wendy's lack of enthusiasm. She then inquires, "Wendy, you're so enthusiastic. So, what is a youth ambassador?" Wendy throws both hands up as she answers, "I don't even know... and I tried to use that as a good reason ..." Amber cuts her off in order to explain in details. She finishes Wendy's statement, "But Pastor

Wynn was not hearing no excuses. Youth ambassador means that Wendy will serve as our youth leader and represent our youth ministry in our national church organization."

She begins to celebrate with some dance moves and sort of singing, "Our youth ministry going to be lit..." Gurley asks, "Lit?! You mean like hell fire lit?! Wendy immediately snaps at Gurley. There is an attitude of grudge directed at her as she speaks, "No, that's the type of 'lit' you'll experience for all eternity if you don't..." Martha Lee cuts Wendy off, "Well, it's about time you take on some leadership roles among your peers..." Amber is spilling with joy as she encourages her friend, "Wendy, you can do this. Besides, it's going to be a good experience. I'll be right by your side helping you." Martha Lee continues, "... and I hope you'll put your all into it! Now... who will help with the lemonade? It needs to be poured into the serving container and the ice dropped into it." Amber volunteers herself and Wendy, "We will, Mom! Come on, Wendy! Hop to it, hop to it..." Wendy wittingly responds, "Hey, shouldn't I be telling you what to do? I'm the newly appointed leader..." Amber is both excited about her friend's assertiveness and amused at her wit. She responds, "Okaaaay, way to go... but don't get the big head now... stay grounded, Wendy.

It's only lemonade..." They all laugh as the doorbell rings. Wendy asserts her newly found leadership skill again as she instructs her aunt saying, "Get the door, Aunt Gurley." Aunt Gurley is not hearing all that. She responds without budging, "Look now, little niece, I'm not your peer." They all share a laugh as Wendy throws her hands up and makes her way to the door. It's Savannah.

Savannah steps in. She greets Wendy, "Hello, Wendy. I'm happy to see you're in great spirits... I've been kinda worried about you ever since I heard you got suspended from school. You okay? Hello Amber, my beautiful niece. Hello y'all. Martha Lee, how you doing? Just dropped by to say hello; really." Martha Lee speaks in a joyful voice, "Well, you're just in time... we got a big shin-dig going on in just a few minutes and you're invited." Savannah cuts a two-step move and shouts, "Well, hey now! Let's get this party started!" Just as they begin to laugh and celebrate, the doorbell rings again. Wendy answers the door to Vera, April, Mae and Junie.

Without speaking, Mae makes a beeline to the couch and plops down with her arms crossed. She's clearly very angry about something. With a tinge of embarrassment in her demeanor, Vera greets Martha

Lee, "Hello again. See, it took no time at all." Martha Lee is willing to overlook Mae's teenage attitude in order to put her guest at ease. She beckons Vera and the rest of the family, "Yes, I see. Come on in." They all move inside the house and Junie brings the attention to himself. He takes center stage, taking on the persona of a pint-sized gentleman. "Hello, Ms. Martha. It smells like, like, like ... good food... is that fried chicken I smell?"

Everyone laughs as they begin to gather at the buffet area, but Martha Lee takes charge. "Let's say grace before we dive in. But first, Wendy, go escort your Pop-Pop from his room to dinner and get the boys as well." Everyone else gathers around and bows their heads as they ready themselves for prayer. That is, except for Mae. Martha looks at Mae, and then at Vera. Vera gets that Martha is requiring everyone to join the circle. Vera admonishes her daughter, "Mae! Get over here." Mae doesn't budge. She continues to sit on the couch by herself with her arms crossed, sulking. It's awkwardly quiet.

Wendy and the boys, along with Pop-Pop in tow, return. Vera continues with Mae. This time, she raises her voice to give one directive. She says, "Now!" Mae still does not budge. It's even more awkwardly quiet.

At last, Vera makes a move in her daughter's direction. Mae gets up and joins everyone, standing between Wendy and Amber, taking them each by their hands. Martha Lee proceeds with prayer. "Dear heavenly Father, thank you for the food, family, and friends that we are about to enjoy. Bless us and bless the food, in Jesus name. Amen. Well, let's dig in." Everyone moves at once, and for the next few minutes, there is a lot of chattering, laughing and fun chaos as everyone begins to fill their plates with food.

Soon, all are settled in various places throughout the kitchen and dining areas. The boys settle in their corner of the living room with their PlayStation game. Frankie and Eric are first up so they each cover their ears with their headphones, while Junie waits for the next game, happily chewing on his chicken and forking down his mac and cheese. Pop-Pop sits in his rocker nibbling on his food. Wendy, Amber and Mae settle in the living area on a couch, as they did the night before. Amber speaks first, resuming the conversation they were having before the guests arrived, "So Wendy, have you thought about your vision for the youth ministries for this year?" Wendy exclaims, "Amber... I was just appointed two hours ago... but I have been thinking about ways to get out of serving..." Mae chimes in on the conversation. She says, "Wait, you mean youth ministries as in Jesus, Christians, holy tongues and all that?!" Wendy and Amber give Mae a blank stare.

Oblivious of their attitudes, Mae continues. "... The Bible... Sunday school, ... listen... who got time for all that?! We are too young to be giving God and the Holy Jesus Spirit any time of our young lives ... we got better things to do." Offended, Wendy and Amber ask the same question at the same time. They say in unison, "Like what?!" Mae retorts, "Like what?! I have to spell it out for you? Like going with boys and being free. Giving them what they want... you know like..." She stops talking to make an inappropriate sexual gesture. She sees that neither Wendy nor Amber is impressed. Frustrated, she begins to complain, "Don't tell me that my new best friends are goody-two shoes."
There is another awkward moment.

Meanwhile, Mae's sexual gestures have gotten Savannah's attention from across the room, and she begins to approach the teenagers. Mae continues without noticing Savannah approaching them, "... Great! My new best friends are virgins..." None of the girls notice that Savannah is now standing far enough away from them to not be noticed, but close enough to hear their conversation. Mae continues to rant, "... I have a lot of work to do with you two. Hey, how can we break out of this joint?" She looks over her shoulder, "Is there a backdoor we can slide out of? Either of you has a car?"

She reaches for Amber's phone and begins to dial before Amber has a chance to object. Amber addresses Mae's conduct in a sincere and sympathetic manner. She says to her, "Mae, you need Jesus... Have you ever..." Mae puts her finger up to let Amber know that she needs to hold her thought as someone is answering her phone call. She speaks into the phone with vigor, "Hey Ray, what up? You out tonight?... You hanging with Jack Daniels and the, ah what they call him?!... that's right, the Dope?"

While Wendy and Amber are flabbergasted and speechless at Mae's audacity, Savannah is not. She snatches the phone from Mae and begins to plead with her with womanly wisdom. "Mae, is it?! Do you know how beautiful and valuable you are? Your life is worth more than you think. Trust me on this, you don't want to go down this road..." Mae viciously cuts Savannah off, yelling at her, "Lady, I don't know who you are, but I'm not the one! I need my phone back... and I do know how beautiful I am and I know how much I can get! Been there, done that... can teach you a thing or two..."

Savannah catches herself from firing back. With this, there is silence in the house while everyone takes a moment to process what they've just heard. Vera finally finds her voice and addresses Mae. She says in a stern, threatening tone, "Mae, for the last time, you've embarrassed me... if you don't get your butt up right now and apologize to this grown adult woman, I will..." Mae defiantly cuts her mother off, "What?! What? You gonna make me go sit in the car? Send me home to sit in my bedroom?" Junie, says, "Girl, you don't have a bedroom..."

Vera loses her patience with her children and raises her voice at Junie before raising her hand to slap him. Her open hand catches his shoulder, missing his cheek by a mere inch as she shouts, "Shut up, Junie! And go sit down! Matter of fact, gather up your things. We need to get going! I'm sorry, Ms. Martha, but..." Mae continues with her defiance, "Where are we going to go?" A desperate Junie begins to plead with Martha Lee. He gets her attention by standing in front of her and unintentionally looking her square in the eyes. With one hand on his hip, he speaks, "Ma'am, can I have a to-go plate? All that chicken doesn't need to go to waste. You have something to put it in?"

By this time, Vera is beyond angry. She turns her frustration to Junie and then to Mae as she hangs onto one of April's arms, causing one side of the toddler's body to dangle in mid-air. She raises her voice, "Junie, boy!! Go stand over there by the door." She softens her voice to address Martha Lee, "I'm sorry, Ms. Martha Lee. All y'all. We are going to be going home right now. Forgive us." She hardens her voice as she yells at Mae, "Mae, get yourself up and apologize for your behavior to this woman right now so we can be on our way... you hear me? I will hurt you. Think I won't? Don't try me, girl."

Without moving a muscle, Mae flippantly answers her mother, "Apologize for what?! You the one need to be apologizing... got us out here, like..." Feeling a strong urge to protect his mother from his sister's accusations, Junie snaps at Mae, "It's not her fault that we have to live in our car, Mae!" At this, Vera loses her last bit of composure. As everyone spectates with disbelief and bewilderment, Vera attempts to regain control over her children's mouths. Martha Lee relieves her of April's arm, as she gently picks up the child and begins to cuddle her.

"Junie, shut your mouth." Vera shouts, "Boy, you're going to make me hurt you." She grabs her handbag and makes a beeline for Mae's arm, and then the door. Gurley speaks under her breath to Savannah who's standing next to her, "This boy is off the chain; the family off the chain..." Mae allows her mother to pull her across the room towards the door. But, she doesn't stop her mouth from spilling the dirt on her family. She continues to disrespect her mother.

She says, "Whose fault is it then?! Andre was a good stepfather, until..." Vera becomes enraged as she answers her daughter, "He was always a bad man; we just didn't know it until you started strutting around sniffing yourself!" Mae begins to laugh and taunt her mom. She says, "You're going to blame me because you couldn't keep your man?!" Still holding onto Mae's arm, Vera says, "Girl, you need to shut your mouth before I shut it for you ... you little tramp..." Vera balls up her fist and raises it in order to physically attack Mae, but then catches herself. The room is completely still and quiet, except for Frankie and Eric who continue to enjoy their game completely oblivious to the shenanigans because of the headphones they're wearing.

Vera uses a long painful moment to regain her composure before making her departing speech. With angry tears welling up in her eyes, she says, "I'm sorry for ruining the evening. Thank you so much for the food and time..." But Martha Lee pleads with her. "But, where are you going to go? Hold on, let's see what we can do. You and your children shouldn't ..." Still holding April, she stops herself mid-sentence in order to adjust her tone to a sincerer one. She speaks to Vera again, this time with more compassion. "Listen," she says, "You four are welcome to crash here on our couch for the night until we can see what we can do and how we can best help you in the long run ..."

Both Wendy and Gurley inconspicuously make objections through their body language and whispers under their breath, even though there is no need for them to be concerned. Humiliated, Vera will not even entertain the idea of imposing on Martha Lee's family. "Nonsense," Vera says, "We are fine... we'll be going now!" Junie interrupts, "Well I'll …," but his mother shuts whatever his thought is down. She says to him, "Junie, now I said we are leaving. Now, be quiet." "I was just going to ask for that chicken, Mom," he says. Martha Lee carefully lets April down to the floor in front of her. "Well, wait just a moment. No sense in letting it go to waste." She hurriedly goes to the kitchen, grabs an oversized plastic bowl, and fills the bowl with all the chicken before placing the lid on the bowl.

Gurley looks as if she's going to have a heart attack, and Wendy softly elbows her in order to put her on notice that she's doing a little too much. While Gurley is grieving the departure of the chicken, Junie receives the chicken with glee. Afterwards, Vera hastens her children out the door and closes it tightly after herself. Martha Lee, Wendy, Gurley, Amber, Savannah are all stunned silent for a moment. Pop-Pop, whose been quietly sitting in his easy chair, breaks the silence. "Be warned," he says before quoting, "What you see and what you hear depends a great deal on where you are standing. It also depends on what sort of person you are." He waits a moment as if he's allowing the words of warning to settle in the minds of each hearer. Then he says, "C.S. Lewis said that." There is another lingering moment of awkward silence.

After which, Wendy breaks the silence, "Well, what just happened?" Martha Lee responds, "A tragedy." Gurley chimes in, "Well, I would say, we just escaped a tragedy!" She turns to look at Martha Lee, "What would have happened if she agreed to stay? She and her children... the boy is off the chain and the girl is... OFF DA CHAAAAAIN." With worry and disbelief in her voice, Savannah says, "Should we be calling child services about now?!... But that girl was about to make me lose my salvation or sobriety or both... She enough to make somebody drink and cuss." Wendy chimes in, "But seriously, Mom. What were you thinking to do with us? I sleep here in the living room and Gurley and the boys sleep in my room!"

Martha Lee interjects, "Now, Wendy and Gurley, come on ... The Lord would have made a way. That family is in deep trouble... we ought to care about what the Lord cares about!" Shaking her head out of pity, Savannah says, "I will say, that's the truth... about the trouble they are in... that girl..." Rather than pity, Wendy takes a more pragmatic perspective. She attempts to appeal to the sensible side of her mom. She says, "But Mom, you can care about people, but we don't have to take in every stray and get involved with every crisis. People are messy. That's why I wanna stay out of the way of people. Don't let them too close. That way, you don't learn their business, and therefore, you are not compelled to help. We really didn't have to have them over again this evening."

She turns to Amber to give her specific instructions. "Amber, if we see Mae at school on Monday, let's just look the other way and don't make out like we know her. She is out of control and I refuse to invest my time, energy and good name on someone who is buck wild. I want to stay low, finish school and be about Wendy's business... That is all!" Martha Lee is appalled at Wendy's callous indifference. Attempting to shame her, she scolds Wendy, "Wendy, did I raise you to be this cold?... Girl!" Gurley speaks with the same selfish mindset, "I hear you, Mamma, but Wendy got a point. What are you gonna do with more house guests?" Martha snaps back, "The same way we do with you, Gurley?"

Gurley responds with indignation, "What you mean? I'm not a house guest, I'm ..." But Wendy cuts her off, finishing Gurley's statement, "Homeless... a stray..." Gurley argues with Wendy, "I'm not homeless..." "Oh, yeah? Where do you live then?" Gurley responds, "Here, with..." Wendy cuts Gurley off, proving her point, "Exactly!" Martha Lee steps in to put an end to their bantering, "Alright, you two. We've had enough drama for the night..."

## *Chapter Six*

## Everyone is at Risk of Something

Mrs. Stance and Brandon are standing alone in the classroom moments after Journalism 201 has ended. Brandon, who is highly upset about her choice for this year's yearbook staff, tries to convince Mrs. Stance that it's not too late to change her decision. Mrs. Stance continues to stand her ground because, in reality, she doesn't have a choice since Principal McClain has convinced her to help with teaching Wendy Brown an important lesson on leadership.

Frustrated by Brandon's persistence, Mrs. Stance attempts to close this one-sided debate. "Brandon, there's absolutely nothing you can do or say that will change my mind. My decision to appoint Wendy Brown as this year's editor-in-chief is final. Now, I've done it; it's final." Brandon is unyielding to a fault. He continues his debate, "But, Mrs. Stance, you really don't understand. This is a tragedy. I was made for the job. I've waited my entire high school career for this moment. I've groomed myself for the opportunity. I have a vision for this year! Did you even read my resume and proposal?" Mrs. Stance exaggerates, rolling her eyes to the back of her head, "Remember, I gave it back to you? At which time, I told you the editor-in-chief position does not require a resume. Again, I have appointed Wendy Brown to the position."

Brandon strongly objects, "But, Wendy doesn't even want the job! Neither does Chrissy want to be her assistant... which I even doubt that either of them is capable and even knows what an editor-in-chief does...." Mrs. Stance overcomes his objection, "This is why we have the entire class also working on this project." She stops for a few seconds, and then begins to talk with intrigue in her voice, as if she's just thought of a great idea. She continues, "Here's what I recommend that you do, Brandon. Get in touch with Wendy and pitch your vision to her; think collaboration." She puts on her huge plastic smile, carefully puts both hands on each of Brandon's shoulders, and begins to steer him to the door as she continues, "Now, you're wearing me out! Please go..." Brandon falls for the 'great idea'. "Okay, Mrs. Stance. I guess that's my next best option. I'll let you know how it goes." Mrs. Stance quickly retorts, "Yeah, I'm sure that won't be necessary. Goodbye now."

Brandon disappears into the hallway with an upbeat attitude. Mrs. Stance turns to greet the adults that are beginning to arrive for their recovery meeting. Marguerite and Savannah are the first to arrive. Marguerite begins to grab a few chairs to put into a circle, while Savannah sets the platter of brownies she's carrying on a nearby table. Savannah is the first to speak, referring to Mrs. Stance by her first name, "Hello Barbara, how did your... was it the yearbook committee meeting? Right?" Barbara answers, "Yes, Lord!" And then, she laughs. Savannah, a bit confused, responds, "That bad or that good, huh?!"

Before Barbara can respond, Savannah changes the subject. She says, "On a more serious note, you have a Mae.... uh, what was that last name? Nope, I can't remember her last name... but..." Barbara responds, "No, I don't recall a Mae in any of my classes. What's your point, though?" Savannah continues, reflecting on the past weekend's shenanigans, "Well, it's just that. These kids today... I don't know. They have it pretty bad all the way around, if you ask me. The things some of them are subjected to in this day and age."

Catching on to where Savannah is headed with her thoughts, Mrs. Stance weighs in with her own thoughts. She says, "Yep, that's the truth. Everything from so-called recreational drugs, blatant promiscuity, and even the idea that you don't have to have an education to become successful ..." Savannah interjects, "... and it might be true for some that you don't need an education, but you do need common sense... or some kind of sense... and some kids are under a false sense of rightness, thinking their bad behaviors are acceptable."

Barbara retorts, "Probably because of how accessible bad influence and bad information is. Right at their fingertips via internet, social media, cell phones, their peers and the devil, girl... and there is little to no accountability." "Yes, ain't that the truth," Savannah exclaims. "Some parents are too young and inexperienced, or too overworked and underpaid, or too old to keep up with these ever-changing social trends, or frankly, bound by the laws of this land in order to effectively correct their children and keep them on the straight and narrow." "Exactly," says Barbara, "The last thing a parent wants is for the Department of Children and Families to get involved."

Savannah continues, "Some of these kids... they think they're smart... but really, they're dumb, just dumb." Savannah changes her tone to a more serious one as she continues, "You know, it makes me pause to think... what would a High School yearbook really look like if it reflected a day in the life of some of these 'at risk' kids?" Barbara agrees and her tone is just as serious. "You have a point... and nowadays, every kid is at risk... for something."

By this time, those attending the recovery meeting are ready to begin. Marguerite approaches the two women. She briefly greets Barbara with a smile, and then turns to Savannah and says, "Excuse me, but it's that time." Savannah turns to see that there is a nice-sized group ready to begin. "Oh yes, it sure is." She finishes her thoughts with Barbara, "Anyway Barbara, at the rate some of these kids are going... if they don't escape harsher things... many will end up here." She turns and walks away before Barbara can answer.

Barbara picks up her belongings and hastily exits with a thoughtful look on her face. Savannah joins the group as Marguerite begins, "Good evening, everyone. Let us stand and say the serenity prayer. They all rise and begin to recite the prayer, saying in unison, "God, grant me the serenity to accept the things I cannot change, courage to change the things I can, and wisdom to know the difference. Amen."

As they all take their seats, Marguerite continues, "Tonight, I want us to review steps four and five. Remember, last meeting, we left off at step four, which states, *'Made a searching and fearless moral inventory of ourselves.'*" If you have not done so, I would encourage you to find a sponsor." Joseph asks, "What, may I ask, do we need with a sponsor?" Marguerite turns her attention away from the group and speaks directly to Joseph. "So, a sponsor is an accountability partner. Someone who will walk you through all of the recovery steps."

Before he can respond, Alexis adds to Marguerite's explanation, "... and a person you can call when you're tempted to smoke that blunt. My sponsor talks me off that cliff every day... morning, noon, and driving home from work! She be reminding me of the 'blunt' reality of going back to the way it used to be." Alexis chuckles at her own wit while Joseph, missing her pun, changes the subject. "Excuse me, but if you don't mind me asking, how long have you been sober?"

With a more serious tone than before, Alexis answers by speaking to the entire group, "I'm approaching a year in a few months ... Daily, I struggle. Not so much with the using part... it's the daily living that sometimes gets the best of me. You know, dealing with the consequences of long term drug use." Savannah chimes in, "Right?! A neglected life! I started using in my teens. I was self-medicating... my ailment was mental and especially emotional pain from sexual abuse, abandonment issues and an evil mother."

Savannah continues after a brief pause, "I've finally gotten to a point where when I remember my childhood, I can see some semblance of light in otherwise very dark areas. If y'all only knew my story... back then, starting at around age nine, I was cast into some heavy situations that I was not ready for. I began using drugs to numb me from the pain of feeling and thinking..." She raises her eyebrows and continues, "They tell me that's called 'self-medicating.' Back then, I didn't have a hero who I could go to for help." She turns her attention directly to Joseph and says, "You see, in sobriety, we are encouraged to feel and think through the pain, rather than numb ourselves. Jesus is my hero, and while I'm learning to do this walk with Him, I have a human, my sponsor, who can help me rationalize and navigate ..."

David interrupts, "Yep, Jesus said, 'In this world, you shall have tribulation, but be of good cheer, for I have overcome the world.' He's the hero who saves the day!" Just then, Bill, with a sour look on his face, begins to complain, "This is my last court-ordered meeting... and I will be so glad, Ms. Marguerite, when you sign this paper. In my opinion, these meetings are for people who want to whine about how crappy life is and whimper about how unbearable their childhood was..." He glares at Savannah, and then quickly turns his attention to David and continues, "Oh yeah, and idealize "Christian living."

The room is stark quiet. It's apparent to everyone that Bill is either drunk or high off drugs. Notwithstanding, his rude behavior, slurred speech, clammy skin and bloodshot eyes are all dead giveaways. After a moment, Joseph timidly speaks to Bill, "That's all you get from these meetings?" He looks around the room at the group, and then speaks to them all. "Thank you for sharing. I've been in just a few meetings and already, I've heard, on a very personal level, reasons why I need to be here." There is silence again.

Finally, Marguerite clears her throat and resumes the meeting saying, "Savannah, please read step five." Savannah picks up a large blue book, flips through a few pages and begins to read from it, "Step five, 'Admit to God, to ourselves, and to another human being the exact nature of our wrongs.' Oh, this is a good topic because it challenges us to confront the truth and embrace humility." With a lighter tone, Marguerite chimes in, "Of course, after we've made that list of our character faults, we don't get off the hook by getting to keep all that truth to ourselves..."

Alexis cuts her off to say, "It's sort of like how repentance and confession works. This is how my sponsor explained it to me. When we are ready to be honest and face the truth about ourselves, we come to God with a changed mind about how we want to live and we confess every bit of wrong we've done. This shows that we are willing to acknowledge it." She thinks out loud to herself, and then continues, "What else did she say? Oh yeah, when we confess, God then forgives us, and then takes the weight of sin from us... so when we confess to a sponsor..." Bill, ruder than earlier, interrupts her thoughts, "See, this is what I mean... why I got to tell someone else my business?! I was raised that my business is my business!"

Sighs, moans and grumbling under the breath can be heard throughout the group, but everyone knows from personal experience that it's not wise to get into a debate with a drunk. David responds to Bill's rude outburst with the utmost respect and patience. Making a point to establish direct eye contact with Bill, he says, "That may be true. However, when we've been completely honest with another person, it confirms that we have been honest with ourselves and with God... the Bible does say, 'Confess your faults one to another...' That's in James 5:16." Bill coarsely responds, "I don't have any faults ... especially none that affects others..."

Fed up with Bill's rude drunkenness, Savannah immediately responds, trying to maintain control over her impatience, "Man, why are you here, then?" She answers her own question, "Court-ordered... you must have..." Marguerite quickly cuts Savannah short, "Savannah, let me remind you that we're not here to debate. Everyone comes to these meetings under different circumstances ... and baggage." Savannah tries to make a case for debate, "At some point, though..." She sighs out of frustration, then continues, "Bill, you say this is your last meeting, but you'll be back... if not to this one, to some other one..."

Bill raises one finger as he speaks, "Well, I'm doing just fine with the company that I keep... me, myself and I..." David prudently responds, "Yes, but we have to be careful with that..." He turns to the group and explains, "Isolation can keep you separated from reality..." He spontaneously nudges his head towards Bill as if he were his explanation point. Marguerite expertly moves the focus back to a more diplomatic conversation, commenting on David's last statement, "Yep! I thought I was doing alright! You know, just me and the Lord and my secrets. But, I've learned that isolation can actually keep you isolated from God's perspective." The look on everyone's face prompts Marguerite to elaborate on this last statement.

She continues, "You think you're hearing His counsel, but in truth, you are only hearing and relying upon your own warped desires... calling it God. When we talk to others, we get feedback, and that helps us to know the difference between our own warped perspectives and what the truth really is." She spends a moment to reflect, and then thoughtfully says, "I just wished I'd learned this truth much earlier. I think I could have saved myself some years from suffering in silence and in secret."

"Yes," says Savannah. "I used to feel sorry for myself when none of my family wanted me around... I mean, here I was living in a rat hole, struggling ... meanwhile my sister has this beautiful life. She never wanted me around. Her house is so big that if I did move in, there was a good chance we would have never crossed paths." Everyone chuckles at this. Afterward, she begins to explain, "I used to think, 'Why can't she just love me and accept me as I am?' Rejection hurts, you know?! When I was invited to family gatherings, it always ended badly, further convincing me that my sister resented the fact that I was a part of her family. My viewpoint was that she was an evil, selfish, and hateful witch that took pleasure in torturing me."

Savannah takes a quick moment to soften her voice, and then continues, "In reality... while I was getting high, she was busy working and building an honest lifestyle. The rat hole I lived in was by choice. When I was invited for holidays or family gatherings, I showed up high. The drugs and lifestyle was what she rejected, not me. My truth today is that lifestyle itself was not making my life unmanageable... it was the drugs and alcohol. And today, I'm able to admit this truth to God and to others. I keep away from any lies. Lies give you somewhere to hide." Savannah gives a nod at the group to signify that she has made her point.

At this, Alexis chimes in with a quick twist of the neck and snap of the finger, "Okay ... Oprah, Iyanla or Dr. Phil can't fix my life..." She changes her voice as if she's preaching a powerful sermon, and continues with her thought, "... only God can! So, I had to make the decision to call on Jesus, for real though ... for myself and ... can I get a witness..." Savannah cuts her off to say, "The witness... ah, that would be your sponsor." David agrees, "Yep, We've got to come out of the closet ... tell on ourselves and tell the truth, the whole truth and nothing but the truth... May I say a few thoughts about this step?" Marguerite enthusiastically responds, "By all means. Have at it."

David takes a slow moment before speaking in order to make an impact with his next words, "This step can be an ego deflator. Especially, if you really clean house on your secret thoughts. There is something about coming clean out loud and honestly with someone other than yourself..." Just as he's about to qualify what he's saying, Bill interrupts. "This is NONSENSE! Y'all talking all this gibberish!" He speaks directly to Joseph, "It doesn't take all that, trust me!" He gives an exaggerated eye roll to the group, and then turns back to Joseph, "... tryin' to brainwash people is all..." His voice trails off to silence, creating an awkward moment.

After sitting in the much needed silence, David becomes the voice of reason again. "You know, many years ago, I went to this high school... seems like yesterday. I was the big man on campus, a winner. Football star with alright grades, poised for a full-ride scholarship to the State University... and had all the ladies... yep, I said to one 'Bark' and she barked, to another 'Go fetch' and she'd fetch." He drops his head as he continues his speech, "... mid-senior football season, spinal cord injury... when it finally sunk in that I was never going to play ball again, some years had crept by. By that time, I was in a marriage of convenience, had two kids, a minimum wage job... the glory was gone, and I hadn't even noticed... I was no longer the big man on campus, but a drunk and a lowlife and a two-bit hustler ..."

He continues with his life lesson as he throws his hands up in the air to express the absurdity of his 'reality' back then. "I was 'too big of a star' for junior college. If I couldn't have it all, I guess I didn't want none of it... so instead of football, the streets, weed and the bottle became my ego boosters." He takes a look around the room, lingering his stare on each person before he continues, "I found sobriety in prison... or, I should say, it found me. There, I woke up from a bad dream only to realize how many lives I'd infringed upon—how I abandoned my daughters and wife when they needed me the most."

He stops for a moment to make sure he's been given the grace from the others to continue with his story. Something about their silence and commanded attention permits him to continue. He chuckles, "Of course, I have to give credit to Scratch... that man read me! When I listened to his story, I heard my story—all of it and then some... except for the murder part... but, I don't know. Sometimes, I think what I did to my ex-wife and kids is no different than murder..." He drops his head in shame as he continues, "... and it was his candid willingness to tell his story, transparently. He used to say, 'I can tell you about the bad I did, the women I abused, the hatred I inflicted... who I used to be because, I'm no longer that person.'"

David continues with a hint of emotion in his voice, "I mean, here was this huge man, tattooed, battle scars, lived a hard life... based off of his physical appearance alone, he could have said one word to dictate a prison riot. Instead, he used his influence to help others find the peace that he had. It was incredible to me. Scratch was serving a life sentence for killing his woman and stepchildren in a jealous drunken rage, yet, he lives free... and, I might add, with an enormous amount of remorse and regret, he's free. I wanted what he had." David pauses for a moment, and then continues, using his fingers on one hand to number the list of things Scratch had that he wanted.

He begins with his index finger, "This was his reality, prison deflated his ego, he found God, then found forgiveness, forgave himself... and I guess you could say freedom found him..." He sits with his hand on full display, fluttering all five fingers in the air before adding the moral to the story, "... this is what I've learned... getting your ego deflated is a surefire way to get connected with God, and then begin to really win in life... I'm over twenty years sober because I encountered another man's transparency."

The group is all quietly reflecting on David's words when Marguerite hesitantly breaks the silence. She softly speaks, "What got me sober... the first three steps of the AA program ... but if I wanted to stay sober, I had to commit to step four and five...and the rest, all the way through twelve—all the while, trusting God! But step five? Now, step five brings you home in the Master's presence. There is something about owning your truth that gives you peace with yourself and others, and peace with God." Joseph, who has been writing profusely, interjects, "But, I'm slightly lost... what is it that we are actually doing in step four that we share with the accountability person in step five?"

Marguerite seems to be delighted to lighten the mood with her answer, "It's like stopping to smell the roses. Some of the roses smell wonderful, but some don't smell all that great. In step four, we are writing the story of our lives as if no one will ever read or hear of the story. We write the good, bad and the ugly truth... details of whatever was embarrassing, your past experiences, crisis. In this instance, the bed of roses is your life. As we begin to put it on paper, we begin to really get in touch with what we're thinking and feeling, and when we are feeling it and thinking it ... and we begin to ask God why or when or how. He begins to show you about you, and how it correlates to your bed of roses."

"Right!" Savannah reiterates what Marguerite has explained, "Yeah, you know, like what you've been through in life that has something to do with who you've become or how your past actions have affected others..." David chimes in, "Yes, in this analogy, I suppose the bad-smelling roses could be what we have identified as our deficiencies and character flaws that have brought harm to ourselves and others. Like pride, dishonesty, selfishness and, of course, the root of all evil... pride. Oh, I said that already!" With this, they all laugh, except for Bill. He interjects loudly and with slurred speech, "Well, what is that good for? I tell you, it just gives people license to always be blaming you for what happens... that's what it's good for! Please!"

David responds to this last comment with annoyance, rather than patience, "In our sobriety, we can know what our weak propensities are so that when the people we love start acting like we've done something to them, we can readily understand that more than likely, we are the problem more so than them ... either way, what we understand about ourselves helps us to engage in healthier relationships."

"Or maybe, like in my case," Marguerite says, "What I discovered about myself is that I actually had a lot of resentment and bitterness towards my mom, grandmother... all the women in my family. There were no men in my family, so I was raised by strong, overbearing successful business women. My grandmother still brags about how, on the day her business license from the state was approved, she left her day job and never looked back." She shakes her head as she remembers, "Every time I visit her, I have to hear the long version, which includes a speech on why failure is not an option for us Norman women."

Marguerite throws her hands up as she exclaims, "Well, I don't have a business, YET, so does that make me a failure? In their eyes, probably! It could be my imagination, but I believe pride is a stronghold in my family." She speaks directly to David with a chuckle, "I identified pride as the root of all my evils; that's a fact! And baby, let me tell you, pride has made for some rough times, both in the workplace and outside of it. I took to drinking because I was beginning to feel like a social misfit, which only escalated my prideful behavior."

With childlike wonderment in his voice, Joseph says, "Wow, all that because you stopped to smell the roses?" Marguerite responds, "Yep, we can find out some good stuff about ourselves if we'll just..." Savannah joins with her as they speak in unison, "... stop to smell the roses." They all begin to laugh and talk among themselves. Bill, as if he's determined to disturb the oneness of the group says, "What kinda talk is this...? I mean, now y'all got us smelling stinky roses?!"

Immediately, Alexis speaks up, ignoring Bill's last comment, "After I got a sponsor and began to work the steps, I fiercely made a list of every person I wronged and the wrong that I did to them, including my deceased mom. Because of that list, I'm getting over self... I'm just regretful it took me so long to wake up and see self." She turns to face Bill, but not necessarily to speak directly to him, "Sometimes, the truth about self is difficult to face. Admittedly, this is hard when I think about it, but taking into account how many people I've hurt and made miserable because I was fearful, angry, lazy and selfish, is motivation enough for me to continue in sobriety. Thank God for His truth..."

"Well," says David, "John 8:32 does say that! 'You will know the truth and the truth will make you free!'" Alexis responds, "Right! I just wish these people I work with and all the customers I have to deal with will do their own personal inventory so they can know the truth! The world would be a much better place to live in if this could happen." She lets out a comical whine as Savannah inquires, "What's wrong now, Alexis? What are they doing to my girl? You need me to come down to that call center and set it off? You know I can give them the one, two..." She makes a gesture with her fists as if she's shadow boxing.

"Yes, Ms. Savannah! Yes!" exclaims Alexis. "Today, a customer calls in with a huge attitude." Alexis takes a moment to become an animated character, and then puts her hand to her ear as if she's talking on the phone to a customer. She continues by interchanging her voice to become an irate person, and then back to herself. "'Question!'
'Okay, I'm listening.'
'Why did you add $16.17 to my bill?'
'Okay, I can help you with that, ma'am. Let's take a look. Okay ma'am, that negative sign means it's a credit. Your bill is actually lower.'
'Well, who told you to lower my bill without my permission?!'"
Savannah slaps her forehead and says, "Oh Lord... see people need to know the truth...." Alexis giggles, "Yes, some people are so blinded by their own faults that when you try to help, they bite your hand. They need to stop drinking and come to Jesus!"

There is a laughter that bursts forth from the group. As it continues, the laughter is more expressed as an appreciation to have been relieved from the heaviness of the evening's discussion more so than Alexis' wit. After the laughter begins to diminish, Joseph reflects on the evening's agenda. "Well, I must say that tonight has been very eye-opening for me. I consider attending these meetings well worth my time... I've been sober now officially for exactly seven days. But after what I've heard tonight, I know that in order for me to continue to be sober, I'm going to need a sponsor. So David, could you be that person for me?"

David extends his hand to Joseph signifying his willingness to serve Joseph in this capacity. He says, "See you after we adjourn." He turns his attention to Bill and offers his twenty years' experience of sobriety to him as well. "What about you? You need a sponsor?" Bill, of course, is not so compliant to the program's recommendations of getting a sponsor. He responds with a sour look on his face, "Stop bro... right there... I told you, I'm not tryin' to do this sober thing. I'm not alcoholic." He rises to his feet and begins to move towards Marguerite.

He continues his speech, staggering as he walks, "I'm here because I'm court-ordered to attend ninety meetings in ninety days... and it's none of your business why, so don't ask. Anyway, the point is, I'm done with this in exactly..." He stops for a dramatized moment to look at his watch, then continues, "... two minutes and some odd seconds. Here you go, Ms. Marguerite. Sign this, please, so I can go ahead and leave this all behind me..." As Bill awkwardly stands with his crumpled court documents in his hand, Marguerite stares at him with pity in her eyes. Then turning her attention back to the rest of the group, she says, "And I think we will end on this thought... Why do some alcoholics have to hit rock bottom before handing their lives over to God? Let us rise for the Lord's Prayer..." They all rise and begin to recite the Lord's prayer.

## Chapter Seven

# There's Always Potential for Change

It's been nearly two months since Mrs. Stance, Wendy's journalism teacher, announced that Wendy will serve as this year's editor-in-chief for the publishing of the yearbook. Today is presentation day and Wendy still does not have a plan, nor has she taken the time to meet with her would-be assistants. Frustrated and weary, Wendy is in her usual bathroom stall, trying to block out of her mind the consequences of showing up to class without a plan. She takes her cell phone from her pocket and tries to make a telephone call to the college.

A few girls are congregated in the bathroom as Brandon and Chrissy walk in. Wendy speaks into the phone, "Hello, this is... hello, can you hear me? Hello... this darn reception... they need to put internet in these bathrooms..." She screams into her phone, "Hello!" Brandon and Chrissy trace Wendy's voice to her office stall and begin to knock wildly on the stall door.

Chrissy raises her voice to Wendy from the opposite side of the door, "Hello, Wendy, we know you're in there. We really need to talk to you about the plan for the yearbook. It's been several weeks now already, and we haven't had one meeting..." They both wait for Wendy's response with their ears glued to the stall door. "Go away. I'm busy..." says Wendy. Brandon whispers to Chrissy, "I got this." He then pounds on the door and begins to talk in his over-the-top negotiator's voice.

He begins, "Now Wendy, it's alright if you don't have a vision or know what to do... just come on out and we can talk about it..." He turns to Chrissy and puts his finger to his mouth as they both keep their ears glued to the door, listening. After a moment of silence, Wendy pokes her head out of the bathroom stall. She says, with a bit of disdain in her voice, "Brandon, this is the girls' bathroom... have you no shame?"

"Actually Wendy, you leave me no choice," says Brandon. "I mean, we are all witnesses to what Mrs. Stance said in class about getting our acts together. We are literally down to the wire now, and you're still dodging our efforts to meet with you. Why is this?" Chrissy crosses her arms and chimes in. "Yeah, what you do affects our grade. We need you to pull it together." Wendy quickly snaps back at them both, "Pull it together?! I have more important things to take care of which involves ... more important things... like my future... and I'm fully aware of the fact that what I do affects others and all that, so could you leave me alone while I take care of my... important business...?"

Wendy makes a move to disappear back into her stall office when Mae and two boys loudly enter the bathroom. One of the boys is named Boyd. Boyd is a handsome young man with an athletic physique and an Afro, a hairstyle that makes him look much taller and intimidating than he actually is. And Boyd is holding Mae's hand tightly. He nearly drags her tiny body across the floor as he swiftly moves to the center of the bathroom and stops. "Okay, everyone out. We need this space!" he barks.

Lorenzo, who could be Boyd's clone, except for the fact that he's darker in skin tone, says in a stern voice, "Y'all know the drill; three seconds ... one, two, three..." All the students begin to scurry out of the bathroom except for Wendy, Chrissy and Brandon. They stand looking like deer caught in the headlights of an oncoming vehicle. Lorenzo tries to intimidate them into leaving as he approaches them, "What?! Y'all don't know the drill?!" He stomps his foot and springs his body toward them as he yells at them, "Go!"

Meanwhile, Boyd, who has unzipped his pants with his free hand, proceeds to pull a compliant Mae into one of the bathroom stalls. Wendy, objects to what she knows is getting ready to take place, "Hey, hey, hey, Mae! What's up? You need to leave. I have business to take care of so take that mess to the boys' bathroom." Brandon joins in to object, but his concern is for Mae, "Hey, but are you guys harassing her? Let her go!"

Lorenzo quickly jumps in Brandon's face to challenge him, "What?! You got somethin' to say... you want some of this..." He displays a mean mug, but Brandon is not intimidated.
Lorenzo then makes a sudden lunge at Brandon, which causes him to jump and hide behind Wendy and Chrissy. Wendy continues to admonish Mae, "Oh, my gosh... Mae! I'm not getting suspended again for you... you need to tell your boys what's up..."

At this point, Chrissy gets a great idea and whispers to Brandon, "Get your camera out." Brandon complies as Doris, Jackie and Wander arrive in the bathroom. Doris locks her eyes on Mae, and then on Boyd's unzipped pants. She immediately begins to walk towards them, "Oh no. I know I'm not seeing what I'm seeing..." She turns to her sidekicks, "Girls, you seeing what I'm seeing?"

Jackie speaks on behalf of her friend, "Mae, you know whose man's hand you holding?" At this challenge, Mae quickly adjusts to the hand-holding between her and Boyd to appear more passive on Boyd's part. She snaps her neck and smacks her lips before speaking, "If you were smart enough, you would know I'm getting my hand held." As the girls and guys are having a stand-off with each other, Brandon begins to snap pictures incognito as Chrissy directs him.

With an incredulous amount of arrogance, Boyd says, "Ah Doris, you messing up my mack, baby. You got all of me on tomorrow..." "Are all y'all serious right now?!" Wendy complains. "Football players and cheerleaders... I mean, really; this is a waste of time." Wander aggressively jumps in Wendy's face and says, "No, you're a waste of time. Just go kill yourself!" As Wendy begins to react, a bright flash of light emits from Brandon's camera. The light primarily lands in Lorenzo's eyes since Brandon's camera was pointed towards him at the time of the flash.

"Hey, did you just take my picture? Give me that camera!" Lorenzo lunges toward the camera and tries to snatch it, but Brandon holds on to it as if it's a football, tucking it under his arm and throwing his other arm up to block Lorenzo's attempts. He looks as if he's on the football field making the play that wins the game. "Bro, you don't want your face bashed in. You need to put that camera down before I take it and stomp it!" shouts Boyd, who's still holding Mae's hand as his unzipped pants begin to slide down his hips. Brandon quickly snaps a picture of the two as the school bell suddenly rings out.

Brandon begins to gather his belongings as Chrissy and Wendy do the same when Doris objects, "But wait, take a picture with me and my boo..." She quickly walks to Boyd and snatches his hand up before giving Mae a look that kills. Brandon does not comply with taking a picture; instead, he slips his camera back into its case. Refusing to be deterred, Doris pulls her phone out, flips to the camera and takes a quick selfie. Afterwards, Boyd turns to Mae and whispers something in her ear which makes her smile and shy away. He then proceeds to lead Doris by the hand, and as they walk away, both gangs follow behind them.

Left standing are Wendy, Brandon, Chrissy and Mae. After the gang leaves, Mae's smile slowly fades into a snarl and she barks at the group of kids staring at her. "You see what you did?! You ruined it! Why couldn't you just leave when you were told to?!"
"Wait!" Brandon says with a look of bafflement on his face. "You actually wanted that type of treatment?! It looked like ..." She cuts him off with a contemptuous attitude, "Like what?! No, he wanted me!" The four stand speechless looking at one another.

After a moment, Brandon drops his head as if he's disappointed. He then speaks with a humble, gentle, and apologetic like manner, "I mean this, not in a bad way, but do you wanna try Jesus? I mean, do you wanna come with us? We're going to a revival tonight."
"What?!" Mae exclaims. "Is Jesus going to revive my love life? No, thank you. Been there and done that. Jesus ain't done nothing for me... but give me the blues... move out my way."

She pushes through the group as Chrissy tries to stop her, saying, "Wait, what do you mean?! I used to feel that way, trust me. Whatever happened, whatever you're going through, it will get better... your life is worth more than you know." "Move!" Mae shouts angrily as she storms out of the bathroom. Afterward, there is a moment of speechlessness. Wendy stares at the two for a moment, then finally speaks what's she's been thinking, "Great! Now, I have to hang out with Mr. and Ms. Evangelist... Lord, why?!"

Ignoring Wendy's comment, Chrissy says, "Wow, she's in a dark place. I'm putting her on my prayer list." She speaks to Brandon, "Do you feel like you got some good shots? But, why did you use your flash...?! Man, we could've gotten some pretty interesting images!" Wendy sighs before saying, "What just happened and y'all are worried about pictures?!" Brandon replies, "Well, it's sort of why we've been trying to meet with you. I have a plan for the yearbook. Did you even read my email?"

Chrissy looks at her watch, and then flashes toward the other two, "Well, if you didn't, you're going to have to wing it. We have to get to class and our presentation is due today." She gives Wendy a directive, "Quick, look for that email and begin reading it. Chile, we got to go... come on." Wendy begins to skate through her phone as they begin walking out of the bathroom and down the hall to class.

Wendy, Brandon and Chrissy rush into the classroom, and from there, they hurry to take their seats as Mrs. Stance moves to the front of the class. All of the students are seated except for a few who are still getting situated in their seats. Principal Jean McClain sneaks into the class and takes a seat as Mrs. Stance begins to talk. "Okay, good afternoon, class. We have a visitor for today who will be sitting in to observe today's formalities. Let's welcome Principal McClain." Principal McClain stands and acknowledges the class with a gesture. There are faint greetings coming randomly from the students as Mrs. Stance continues. "We need to get right into our presentation as time is getting away from us. Pretty soon, we'll look up and it will be the end of the year. So, Wendy, you have the floor."

Wendy nervously rises from her seat with her head still buried in her device and begins to move to the front of the classroom. As she walks past where Brandon is seated, he whispers, "You can do this. Just take your time and read everything. It's pretty straight-forward; you'll see." Chrissy chimes in, "You got this, Wendy." Wendy stands alone at the front of the class. She nervously clears her throat and begins to read aloud, sounding like someone reading through a complicated legal document for the very first time.

"As your editor-in-chief for this year's yearbook, I am committed to leading this committee to produce the best and most compelling yearbook of this school's history. The making of a phenomenal yearbook requires organization, teamwork, collaboration and creativity. It's going to take all of us being all in. I'm here to help us stay on point. Consider me as the captain of 'Team Yearbook' and not merely editor-in-chief.'" Wendy sounds a little stiff and a bit hesitant for someone who says they are going to lead a team to victory, and she knows it.

She takes a deep breath and continues to read from her phone, "We will have the usual sections such as Portraits, Academics, Athletics, Clubs, and Student Life. As your editor-in-chief, I intend to make sure we are inclusive this year. And, for this reason, we will have a section called: Student Life 'for real, though.'" She looks at Brandon and discreetly mouths the words "for real, though?" questioning his wittiness. Brandon flashes a proud smile as she continues.

"Inclusive means 'all encompassing, everything included'... student life- 'for real though' will not just include the pretty stuff like the senior prom, homecoming and fashion trends with a photo collage of the best-dressed of the student body. How about we highlight what happens in the day and the life of a not-so-popular student? How about a photo essay layout about what goes on in the females' or the boys' bathrooms, or behind the school during a study hall class? How about some short stories about what type of examples the upper classmen are being to the lower classmen?"

Beads of sweat begin to break out on Wendy's forehead as she considers the magnitude of the words that are coming out of her mouth. "We are journalists, and journalists seek the truth. We're the watchdogs of our school and culture. We have the important responsibility to convey a wise perspective concerning the current events of this school and in the time in which we live... the good, the bad and the ugly, capturing the very fiber of what makes this year unique to all others..." Wendy stops to display a look that says, "What have I got myself into," and then hesitantly continues.

"To do this, we are going to have to make a commitment to get involved with our student body." At this, she just gags on the very words that are coming out of her mouth. Her eyes feel like they are bulging from their sockets as she continues with these words, "We are going to put on our detective hats and

171

become the investigative journalists we are destined to be." She stops again, taking a much needed breath before making up her mind to get through the rest of this unrehearsed speech. "Who knows what truth we will uncover and what lives we'll touch in the process. I am in this world to make a difference. You are in this world to make a difference. Let's take a stand for change. Who's in?" At this, all of the class responds positively. There are random yeses and students shouting either, "I'm in" or "Count me in." These responses can be heard coming from many of the students. Wendy stands in the front of her class with a perplexed look on her face.

Mrs. Stance pops up from her seat with over-the-top glee and a sigh of relief as she speaks, "Well class, or should I say 'Team yearbook,' I think we're off to a good start!" She turns to Wendy and says to her, "... as editor-in-chief, I'm sure the class appreciates that fantastic proposal for the yearbook. It was so motivational and organized." She turns her attention back to the class, "Now, there is much to do so after class, we will take a quick 15-minute break, and then we will all meet right here for our first official planning session."

The school bell rings and some of the students begin to leave the classroom, while others begin to congregate in one area of the classroom. Wendy, Brandon, and Chrissy meet up and begin to walk out of the classroom. "Great job, Wendy. There was nothing better than hearing my vision coming from the lips of another person. Well done," says Brandon. Sounding worried, Chrissy asks, "So... what do we do from here? We have a meeting to lead in about 15 minutes..."

Brandon smiles and answers with glee and a whole lot of confidence, "No worries, the meeting will take care of itself. Did you see how the people responded to the vision?! We got this... so, what do you think, Wendy?" Wendy throws both hands up as she answers, "I'm speechless... No words... just, no words." She looks upward, and under her breath, she speaks again, "Lord, how did this happen... why me, just ... why me?!"
All three leave out the classroom door, passing by Principal Jean McClain and Mrs. Stance as they begin their conversation.

With a look of satisfaction on her face and a hint of it in her voice, Principal McClain speaks to her partner in crime, "Well, would you look at that... this is already turning out better than we had planned. How about that speech?" Mrs. Stance answers, "Now, you know those weren't Wendy's words." Principal McClain enjoys a quick giggle before responding, "Yep, but we got her on the hook committing to them..." As she enjoys another moment of giggling, Mrs. Stance responds, "To be honest, I'm a little concerned about the plan... I mean, really. Taking pictures in the girl's bathroom, the boys... this could get pretty tricky."

"Nonsense, God is all up in this," says Principal McClain, "Do you realize what just happened?! We couldn't have planned for that to happen." Still not fully on board with the plan, Barbara timidly whines, "Yeeeeaah, buuuuut..." Principal McClain loses her patience and snaps back at her friend. "Oh, quit your sniveling, Barbara. It's going to be fine." She puts both hands on her hips and begins to reprimand her.

"Where's your commitment to keeping with this school's vision statement: 'Making today's leaders?!'" She begins to speak in a dramatic voice as if she's narrating an adventure film, "To do this, you have to go out on a limb, take some chances... go into uncharted territories where no school has ever gone before. What better way to do this than in Mrs. Stance's Journalism class where she's teaching students to become those bold leaders that this school can be proud of?"

She gives Mrs. Stance a moment to let the taste of sweet victory settle on her palate, before she concludes her speech with a sharp warning, "Now, when everything goes right, I will be right there to take full responsibility! If anything should go left... uh, this whole idea was yours!!! You got that?!" She cuts her eyes at Barbara, and then quickly gives her a warm reassuring smile. "But, not to worry. God got your back."

A few hours later, the recovery group is underway with the usual group in attendance, and they are in deep discussion. Marguerite expresses herself, "One of the ways to tell if God is in a thing is looking at the evidence of change. If God is in it, you'll see things work out themselves by design; they will just fall into place. Relationships begin to change—they dissolve or evolve effortlessly. An unwanted craving or desire can go away without warning or effort." She waits for a response from anyone in the group.

After a moment, David adds, "And remember, there are no coincidences. If you find yourself in the middle of something important or facing a circumstance that has a potential for change ..." He abruptly stops talking and begins to stare at the person who has just come through the door. Everyone follows David's eyes, which leads them to Bill. They all watch him stagger across the room, take a seat and begin to stare back at the eyes that are watching him. He's obviously drunk. "... or if you're back to the same place you started off in," Savannah says, attempting to finish David's thoughts on 'coincidences'.

But David continues his own thought. As he keeps his eyes fixed on Bill, he says "... it's not by accident. That is, if you find yourself in a circumstance that offers potential for change... there's a part for you to play. Or, at the very least, an opportunity for growth, and until we get it, we'll have to keep repeating it." Marguerite adds, "Doesn't the Proverbs say something about? 'As a dog returns to his vomit, so a fool returns to his folly', or something to that effect...?" "Yep!" David says, "That's Proverbs 26:11." "Well, say that again," says Savannah. "It's important for us who have recovered or are recovering to not shy away from the process... because our lives are still full of purpose. Recovery helps us to be effective ... and stay effective."

Joseph enthusiastically says, "Yes, I have firsthand

knowledge of that... When I started attending this group, I didn't know if my family would survive one household." He clears his throat and loosens his tie, "I've recently realized that I'm an introvert by nature and a perfectionist by choice. What a combination, right?! My excessive drinking... correction, secret excessive drinking drove a major wedge between me and my wife and children. It alienated me from everyday life—well, that and my work schedule. I thought I was a good husband and father, you know. But, I've come to realize that just because I'm able to put food on the table, clothes on my family's backs and a roof over their heads doesn't mean I'm doing it right or that I'm showing up for them." He pauses for a moment of reflection, and then continues.

"I've decided to figure out what being a husband and father really means." He scratches his head and begins to wave his hand around the top of his head. He's trying hard to hide the enormous amount of anxiety he's feeling in this moment of admitting his truth for the first time. "I've found a character flaw—'perfection'—and so, this means, for me, that I can't figure life out by drinking myself into perfection. Quite frankly, I'm scared." He takes a deep breath, exhales, and then continues. "Over these past several months, I've gotten sober. Now, I realize that getting

sober is only half the battle. I'm facing the real battle."
He throws his hands up and continues his speech
with a renewed sense of freedom, using his
outstretched hands to help express himself.

"Relationships scare me... my twins are toddlers and
I've got to figure out a way to empower them on self
love, standing up for themselves, being their own best
friend if they have to and, getting them through their
high school years. Fatherhood scared me into
drinking, and now it's scaring me straight. Correction,
I should say, the prospect of failing my family scared
me straight... and now, I'm left with figuring it out... I'm
scared." He releases his hands to fall on his lap as he
relaxes his body in his chair. "... and I guess that's
okay..."

Bill abruptly says, "Dude, hire yourself a Nanny and
be done with it! One of those Black mammies with the
big bosoms so that when your kids cry, she can just
take 'em in and comfort them, and they can get lost in
her..." Savannah is flabbergasted. "Stop, Bill! Just
stop it! You're getting intolerable now!" says
Savannah. But, Bill continues piercing at Joseph
through bloodshot eyes. "I know who you are,. We all
know who you were... from the first day! These
meetings might be anonymous, but we're not blind.

Your face is plastered over all those billboards in the hood. You have all those businesses. A furniture store on one block, a convenience store on the next ..." He slaps both hands on his knees in order to emphasize his next point, "You have firsthand knowledge that money is the cure-all..."

With disdain in her voice, Savannah says to Bill, "Why are you here again anyway? Oh, I see, ANOTHER court order? I want to know what judge refuses to lock you up..."
Sensing that the discussion is about to go to the far left, Marguerite steps in, "Okay, now that's enough, you two." She looks at Savannah. "Just let it go, Savannah!" But Savannah won't let it go this time; instead, she snaps back, "This is a safe place for us to talk out our issues, but his presence makes us all want to drink!" She talks directly to Bill, "Find another meeting to attend, will you?!"

Alexis chimes in, "He's like the Covid19 virus... a nuisance!" She looks in Bill's direction and barks at him, "Pestilence, be gone! I need a face mask somebody! You, know, you're the person that inspired the creation of the face palm emoji." She slaps herself on the forehead, then continues scolding Bill. "Money is not the cure-all... weren't you listening to the rich

179

man? You're just like the people who call in at the call center... a nuisance!" She fixes her attention back on the group in order to share what's bothering her about her day.

She complains, "A lady today asked me if I had the virus, and then asked if you
can catch the virus from over the phones." She puts her hands up to her ear as if she's holding a phone. "No ma'am, that's the 5G tower's virus!" She laughs at her own wittiness, and then moves on with another story from work. "Another customer calls in saying their Wi-Fi is not connecting to their phone." She once again holds her hand to her ear, "Okay ma'am, I can help you with that." She rolls her eyes to the back of her head, before continuing. "So, I did all the basic troubleshooting I could do in my department. Finally, ma'am, did you check with your internet provider to see if there is an outage?" She then proceeds to say to me, "Internet provider? I don't have internet." Another face palm moment..." David cuts her off, "Um, Alexis, you're digressing..."

Alexis shakes her head in agreement, "I know, I know... but here's the thing..." She takes on a more serious tone as she glances first at Joseph, then at Bill before continuing. "One year ago, I decided that I needed a change... I needed to do more than smoke weed twenty-four seven. My priorities were jacked up... abusing and using people was the name of my game... I was self-centered and selfish. Did you know that I was in line to become a VP at the investment firm where I worked? Instead, for the last year, I've been working at a call center for little more than minimum wage." She drops her head in pity for herself, and then continues, "I landed that job right out of college... I loved it; I was so proud of myself. My hard work had paid off..."

She lifts up her face in order to connect with any person in the group who was looking her way. She finds David's eyes first. "On the day I was escorted out of the building, I was living out of my car... embezzlement—but I couldn't even do that right. Funny thing is, I was trying to handle other people's money, but I couldn't handle my own life. Life has a way of coming full circle, and when that happens, I believe it's God's way of giving us a second chance... it's up to us what we make of it ..." David adds, "Some addicts miss the opportunity to do better... because they die in their addiction before they hit the bottom that will finally wake them up."

Alexis says in a matter-of-fact tone, "Hunty, let me tell

you... I hit rock bottom and that's when I stopped running from the truth. The way I see it is, I'm glad I had to take that call center job. One year ago, I made a commitment to myself to do better. Temperance is sobriety, but it's also restraint..." She chuckles to herself, "One might say that I have learned to restrain from putting my mouth on these people I have to deal with at work. All kidding aside, by the grace of Jesus, I learned empathy, sympathy, honor, patience."

She raises one hand as if she's in a fiery church service and begins to speak as if she were the preacher, "It's a miracle! Today, that lady who didn't have internet—I didn't laugh at her; nope! I didn't get mad because she'd wasted my talk time... I simply said 'Ma'am, you've got to get connected in order to call the main line. You have to have internet, but don't you fret. After you get some, I'll be happy to help you when you call back for help.'" She turns her attention to the group and continues in the same preachy voice, "See, that's because I identified with her. I was trying to do life on my own, but then I realized, I have no connection. I've got to get connected to the one true God if I want to win in this life. If I don't, what's the point?" The group begins to laugh and say "Amen."

"Well, hallelujah," says Marguerite. "I, for one, am very impressed with how you've progressed. Girlfriend, I knew you when you gave yourself over to God and this program, and obviously, it's working for you..." Joseph brings the discussion back to Alexis' job. "So Alexis, you have a degree and a background in finances. Why don't you..." Alexis answers Joseph's question before he can finish it, "... get a better-paying job in my field? Because I also have a criminal background; it's God's grace I got a plea bargain with no jail time, but who's going to trust me enough to hire me?" She shrugs her shoulders in defeat.

Joseph adjusts himself in the chair he's sitting in with ease as he propositions Alexis, "Well, I was going to say, why don't you consider working for me?" There is a moment of silence. Then, Joseph continues in a humble manner, "I forgot my wife's birthday for the third year in a row. I can't imagine missing another special moment in my toddlers' lives. I want to 'stop and smell the roses'... I think it's necessary if I'm going to do better..." He stops to wait for an answer from Alexis. It appears she's too stunned to answer, so he continues, "I need someone who can help me run my companies for a while..." He stops again to wait for an answer.

Alexis replies, "Ah, I just said, I have a criminal background... and..." Joseph cuts her off, "I heard you. But, you also said that God is a God who gives second chances, right?! I happen to believe that about God also! Sooooo...." Just then Bill cuts in raising his hand as if he's a third-grader, and speaking with a drunken slurred voice, he says "Ohhhh, I'll take it if she got to think about it..." An annoyed Alexis shuts Bill's absurdity down, "Ah, can we discuss this after we adjourn?" "Absolutely," says Joseph. "Won't He do it?!" screams Alexis, trying to contain herself. "Won't He do it?!"

David places a hand of congratulations on Alexis' shoulder and says, "Yes, He will! There are no coincidences in God... I've been coming to these meetings now for nearly twenty-five years and ..." Bill interjects, "Wait, twenty-five years?! You haven't learned yet...?!" David very calmly responds, "Son, I HAVE learned. That's why I keep coming back. Someone once said, 'If it ain't broke, don't try to fix it.' Things should only be changed if there are problems with it." His smile diminishes, signifying that what he has to say next is heartfelt.

"Now, I'm not at risk. I will never go back to the way it used to be. For me, every time I step into one of these meetings, I'm reminded that there is a need to tell someone that they too can become an overcomer... I'm a walking and living testimony. Even in our darkest hour, God is there and He will never let you down..."

Savannah agrees, "Yes, it's so true... I still do need to be reminded that I can overcome. You see, it's not the drinking and drugs that have me weak, it's life without them that baffles me sometimes..."

She puts her hand over her mouth to muffle the sound of her voice as she reveals her age. "I'm age fifty something or another and I'm just figuring out life. I'm a full-time student studying psychology so that I can counsel people like Bill..." She begins to laugh as the others do the same, except for Bill. He says, "Hey, I don't need counseling! I need for these judges to leave me alone—is what I need..." Savannah continues, "But seriously, Joseph, I think we all struggle. For me, it's being productive, doing something for myself that I didn't know or think I could do, you know. It's pretty scary sometimes. I, for one, need to be reminded that I can do life without false securities. I just wish that hitting my rock bottom could have been years earlier. I wish that when I was a girl, making that decision to give up on God... there could have been a hero like you, David, that could have just taken me by the hand, looked me in my eyes and got through to me. Tell me that I didn't need the drugs to feel better... that in my darkest day, when I couldn't see light didn't mean that 'the Light' wasn't there... you know? If someone had taken the time to tell that little girl, Savannah, that God is love and don't give up on Him, He will come through and He does care and that there are bad people in the world, and it's not your fault, and you don't have to fix yourself... God will make a way..."

It's quiet for a moment, and then Savannah breaks the silence in a calm voice, "My sister, that same sister who I thought hated me, is fully supporting me. She's paying my way through school and my bills... so that I can focus on sobriety and bettering myself..." She sighs, "I hit my rock bottom and by God's grace, it didn't destroy me." She looks directly at Bill, and then resumes talking. A lot of us don't survive rock bottoms. Because, we don't know that we are actually at our rock bottom. We overdose, commit suicide, or just plain give up on life when we're at our lowest points." She looks away from Bill and puts her focus back on the others. "That was enough for me. My lowest was enough to make me make up my mind. I choose to live. I knew it was time for a change. Go figure. I purposed in my heart for change and God sent the help—a hero ... talk about a God of second chances who sees me! If ever I can be a hero to someone in need, I won't hesitate... I'm going to tell them..."

# Chapter Eight

## Take a Stand for Change

The hallways are filled with a sea of students hustling and bustling past one another. It's the end of the day and the end of a long week of third-semester final exam testing. The sound of metal locker doors slamming shut, loud voices and kids chatting add to the after-school chaos. There is a sense of relief and freedom in the air. Amber, who has been hurriedly navigating her way through the crowds, finally catches up with Wendy.

Amber taps Wendy on her shoulder to get her attention. Wendy looks over her shoulder, and seeing that it's Amber, turns in her direction. With both hands on her hips, Amber begins to admonish her friend, "What's going on with you? For the past few months, I barely see you anymore, and when I do, it seems your mind is somewhere else. I stop by your house and you're never home. In between classes, you're always hemmed up in a huddle with your 'team' or in the bathroom interviewing someone. I get it. The yearbook needs to be published... but what's going on

189

with you goes beyond the yearbook work!" Amber catches herself raising her voice and takes a moment to calm herself.

After a moment, Amber continues with a more sensitive voice. "You're different; we're different... I feel like ... like." Wendy cuts her off to finish her thought, "I care? ... And... it does go beyond the yearbook..." Amber interjects, "Wait, did I just hear you say, 'I care,' Miss 'I don't want to get involved?'" Ignoring the sarcasm, Wendy says, "Amber, did you know that within the past two years in this county alone, there have been twenty-eight child suicides and three have been from this school? Did you know that two girls have gone missing from our school for several months now?"

Amber humbly drops her head, "There's a rumor out ... it's sex trafficking..." Wendy continues, "We are losing our peers at an alarming rate. Let's count the amount of drug use that we know about in this school." Amber shakes her head in agreement, "Our school is a high achievement school... we are supposed to be smart." Wendy says, "Since I've been working on our yearbook project, in these past few months, I've confirmed about a dozen abortions here in Charles T. Turner Tech High ... just in the first half of the year..." The mood has changed to a somber one. Amber says, "No, I didn't know all that ..."

Meanwhile, a line of students of all sorts has formed behind them. As Amber and Wendy continue their conversation, the line seems to be getting longer. Oblivious to this, Wendy continues, "I'm not making excuses for them, you know... bullying, drug use, promiscuity is never okay, but sometimes, the problems seem like a catch twenty-two, you know? ... The bully may have been bullied and probably neglected at home. The girl who gives her body so freely could have been molested or neglected... those that find drugs and alcohol... some crisis at home, dysfunction in family ..." Amber, noticing compassion in her friend's voice that was not there before finds herself speaking with the same passion, "I guess what you're saying is, hurting people hurt people... or themselves."

Wendy shrugs her shoulders and says, "It's the 'stress factor'... Remember, last year when Joey Carter and his crew tried to date-rape me? I escaped by the grace of God. But, that changed me." Wendy speaks as if what she's getting ready to say is something that she's never said out loud, almost as if she's getting the revelation as she speaks., "I stopped caring. I've been living with my eyes wide-shut ever since... until..."

Amber attempts to console her friend, "I guess I get it... but Wendy, you can't' change the world, certainly not in one school year anyway. Just remember, you have a life and a best friend who barely sees you anymore." Wendy lightens the mood with a more jovial voice, "What do you mean, Amber? I see you every week at church, and then again at Youth Night, where you assist me in the endeavors of the Lord. I might add..." As she chuckles at this, Amber says, "Well, that's true, and Youth Night was lit this past week. You're doing a great job." "Why, thank you. Thank you for saying..." says Wendy.

Amber adds, "Yeah, our youth ministry is changed forever. All the guest speakers you're bringing in and the vision statement for this year just lines up with everything about our lives: 'Identity: Take a Stand for Change!' I love it." Just then, an impatient Wander, one of Doris' posse members breaks into their conversation, "Excuse me, Amber, but your time is up." Confused, Amber retorts, "What?! What are you talking about, Wander? My time is up?... girl..." Wander responds with a boatload of sassiness in her voice, "I need to talk to Wendy, please. You holding up the line..."

Both Amber and Wendy look up to see a long line of their peers impatiently waiting. In the same instance, Chrissy and Brandon show up with cameras, notepads and other supplies, and begin to set up their workstation. Perplexed, Amber asks, "The line?!" She looks at Wendy with shock. "Oh no... Okay, Madame counselor... do your thing! I'll catch up with you this weekend. Remember, we need to start planning for a graduation party and our college debut. Oh, did you ever settle that issue with your scholarship for the university?" Wendy whines, "Believe it or not, Amber, it's still an ongoing issue... but we'll talk... this weekend..." "Okay, see you later," says Amber as she leaves.

"Okay Wendy, we need to talk..." says Wander as she throws her hands on her hips and waits for Wendy's response. Wendy responds with a bit of humor, "Okay Wander, but first, can you please tell me where your name came from? I've always WOOOOANDERED about that..." Wendy giggles a little and it seems to help release the tension coming from Wander. She, in turn, giggles a little, snaps her finger, then her neck, and says, "Okay, you coming for my name. Okay, but frankly, I really don't know; they say it has something to do with when I was a toddler and the way I walked or something. On a serious note..." Wendy cuts her off and summons Chrissy.

"Hey Chrissy, google the word "wander" and give me some synonyms." Chrissy grabs her device and begins the research as she walks toward Wendy and Wander. As she reaches them, she begins to read the results. "Yo, it says here... synonyms... meander, walk, roam, mooch, drift, stray... Wow. One of the definitions says here... 'to walk or move in an ... aimless way...'" She stops reading and looks at Wander with pity in her eyes, "Girlfriend... wooooow!"

Wendy takes on a more serious tone when she begins to speak to Wander. "I'm going to speak frankly with you. Now, you're not an aimless follower, but you've been allowing people to call you that every time you answer to the name Wander. What's your birth name?" Wander responds, "Deborah..." "What?!" says Wendy. "Deborah?! Girl, you've been having an identity crisis. You're not a wanderer who just follows aimlessly, you are a Deborah who is full of wisdom, someone who is a courageous leader."

Wendy turns to Chrissy. "Chrissy, google Deborah from the Bible..." Chrissy does so and reads aloud. "Deborah is one of the most famous women of the Bible. Known as a Judge, prophetess and a hero..." Wendy interrupts and says to Wander, "You will become what you allow people to call you. Stop answering to the name Wander and demand people call you by your birth name. Girl... there is a hero in you..." Wander is speechless. She manages to get one word out, "Oh, ..." Wendy comes off of her soapbox to ask the question, "But, what did you need to talk to me about?"

Satisfied with her newfound identity, Wander responds, "Nothing now. I think I got what I came for." She gleefully walks away. Just then, a loud blood-curdling scream can be heard coming from the girls' bathroom. Panic and hysteria immediately follow as Jackie, Doris's other posse member, emerges from the girls' bathroom bearing bad news. "Someone call 911! I think that girl, Mae, is lying dead in the bathroom..."

At this, Principal McClain comes out of her office with her radio and cell phone. She begins calling 911 with one device and issues a staff alert with the other as she rushes through the crowd of students determined to get to the bathroom as quickly as possible. She yells at her cell phone, "We have a life and death emergency at Charles T. Turner Tech High, interior east side of the building, girls' bathroom! We need EMT right away..."

Then, she turns her mouth toward the radio and does the same, "All staff, code 08- girls' bathroom—security to clear the halls...ASAP!" She lowers the device and begins to sternly bark orders at the clutter of students hindering her pathway, "Alright, clear the halls! Clear the halls; evacuate the building! Kids, go home!" she yells.

Through the crowd, Principal McClain catches a glimpse of Doris, who has guilt written all over her face. She yells to her, "You, right there! Young lady—Doris!" Doris responds by raising her eyebrows as if to question whether the principal is talking to her or not. Principal McClain answers the unspoken request by nodding her head up and down, as she speaks in a loud tone, "You stand right there! Don't you move a muscle; you hear me? Not a muscle." Doris looks like a dear caught in headlights as she complies.

Principal McClain throws the radio up to her mouth again, and with both eyes fixed on Doris, she speaks into her radio to address Mrs. Stance. "Barbara, I've got a young lady here in the hallway." She lets the radio down just enough to bark another order at Doris. "You, go stand up against that wall right there. Mrs. Stance is coming for you." She speaks into the radio again, "Barbara, she's standing against the wall here next to the lobby; you'll see her..." She then barks another order at Doris, "Raise your hands and keep them up until Mrs. Stance finds you." She speaks back into the radio, "Detain her, please."

At this point, Principal McClain disappears into the girls' bathroom. Chrissy, Brandon and Wendy are close behind with cameras and microphones in tow. Meanwhile, full pandemonium has broken out. Teachers are hastily escorting kids through the exit doors, and many of them are racing to exit the building for fear of the unknown. The emergency vehicles are arriving and the flashing lights suddenly begin to beam through some of the windows. In just a few short moments, it seems the school is like a ghost town with just a few kids still making their way to the exits as the E.M.T. workers are rushing in with their life-saving equipment.

Doris is left standing alone just as Principal McClain commanded her. She's leaned up against the wall with both arms held high above her head. She looks as if she's about to be arrested. Jackie approaches her, and in response to the look on Jackie's face, Doris pompously responds, "What?! She deserved it!" Jackie quickly retorts, "I'm not going to jail for you." She throws her hands on her hips and snaps her neck as Mrs. Stance walks up to them both. "You two... come with me. Now!" They both stand at attention and begin to follow Mrs. Stance as she leads them in the direction of Principal McClain's office.

## Chapter Nine

## Embrace Newfound Identity

It's been just a few weeks since the incident at the school and Wendy and Amber are at Wendy's house, sitting on the couch with their laptops open. "What do you suppose it means to answer the call to action?" Wendy asks. Amber responds almost immediately, "'Click here,' 'buy now,' or 'sign up'..." "No," Wendy says. "Not on social media or on somebody's business website... I mean... like something in your heart. You think you should do because, now your eyes are open." Amber looks puzzled, so Wendy continues, attempting to explain what she means. "I'm afraid if I don't take action, it might change me... forever... and my eyes will close again..."

Amber asks, "What are you talking about? Does this have to do with Mae's death? You know, they're calling it a drug overdose and not manslaughter..." Shaking her head in agreement, Wendy adds, "She had a mixture of cocaine and opioids; it was laced with Fentanyl, and she had three times the legal limit of alcohol in her system... Coroner ruled that she just stopped breathing..." "Yeah, and you know Doris has to be relieved that she's not facing charges," Amber says in a matter-of fact like tone.

Wendy leads the conversation back to her original thought. "I came across this quote, right?! 'Life is ten percent of what happens to you and ninety percent of how you react to it.' What do you think?" Amber says, "I think something definitely happened to Mae..." Wendy thinks out loud, "How we respond makes the difference..." She gives herself a moment, and then continues her thought, only this time, speaking at Amber. "When Mae died, something happened to me. I mean, before that happened, something was happening to me... but when she died... I feel like I need to take action in some way. I'm just not sure how... and ... why."

There is a moment of quiet reflection before Amber responds, "I think it changed all of us in some way... so close to home, you know..." "What could we have done differently with Mae?" asks Wendy. "That's a good question... I don't think much; she was out of control... marching to the beat of her own drum..." Amber responds. "I know, but, what can we learn from her? Or, how can we do better for hurting or troubled people?" Wendy asks.

As they both sit and ponder Wendy's last question, Wendy's cell phone rings. She signals Amber to answer the phone since it's on the coffee table nearest her. Amber reaches over and answers it by putting it on speaker. Wendy throws her voice towards the phone, "Hello." A voice from the other end says, "May I speak with Ms. Wendy Brown, please?" "This is her..." says Wendy. There is a slight pause during which time Wendy and Amber eye one another as to question what this call could be about.

Finally, the voice speaks again. "Hello, this is the administrator of admissions, Ms. Young. I'm returning your call to inform you that your scholarship discrepancies have been resolved. You can now proceed to early enrollment. You should have received an email confirmation. Meantime, I need student verification ... What is your...?" Wendy cuts Ms. Young off, "Ummm, ma'am. Excuse me, but...." Wendy displays a long agonizing pause, then looks at Amber with an apologetic expression.

"Hello? Hello... I just need your student ID..." Still apologizing to Amber with her eyes, Wendy speaks up, "Umm, I won't be needing... um, can I call you back?" She abruptly hangs up the phone as if she's made a prank call. "What did you just do?" Amber asks. "You've been trying to register now for almost half of the year and..." Wendy says with a great deal of resolve in her voice, "And I've finally realized that that's not what I need to do."

Amber is appalled at what she just heard her friend say. "Not what you need to do? Girl, go to college?! You don't need to go to college?!!" Wendy tries to explain, "Well no, ... I mean, yes—go to college—just not away to college. I've decided to go to State University right here at home... close to... hurting people." Just then, Martha Lee comes through the front door, but neither of the girls notice. Picking up the uneasiness between the two, Martha Lee begins to unintentionally eavesdrop on their conversation.

"Hurting people, girl... There are hurting people at Duke ... all over the world, for that matter..." Amber emotionally exclaims. Wendy remains much calmer. "I know it sounds crazy, but I just feel I can make a difference. Now, I don't have it all worked out yet, but I'm sure I want to do this. This past year has been an eye-opener..." Amber is beside herself with grief, "Wait, you're serious?!" Wendy can only shake her head in affirmation.

As reality begins to set in, Amber is overwhelmed with emotions. Her passion can be heard in her voice as she begins to reason with her friend. "You earned the right to attend Duke! For heaven's sake, Wendy, your GPA is higher than mine. You can be anything that you want to be..." Wendy remains calm as she answers, "I know that, now... and I think I know what I want to do... What I want to pursue." Amber cuts her off, not wishing to hear the alternative to Wendy's education, because hearing it would make Wendy's decision more of a reality to her.

It's something about the calm in Wendy's voice that convinces Amber that Wendy's mind is made up, and this causes her to be filled with emotional anger and disappointment. "We have a plan, Wendy, since eighth grade. We've had a plan and we promised that nothing would stop us! Look at us! We both are accepted to the school of our choice... we are one step closer to fulfilling our dreams... and you're going to throw it all away?" In those next few moments of silence, tears form in Amber's eyes and begin to run down her cheeks.

Feeling guilty, Wendy drops her head, and with a tender voice, regretting what she's about to say, she says, "Friend, it was your dream, your plan, the school of your choice... your journey." She stops to gather the right words in her mind, and then continues with the same tender voice. "All my life, I've felt like I've been on the outside looking in, you know... never fully committed to any one thing ... afraid to give myself permission to be me or let people see me..." She stops to make eye contact with her friend.

"Since eighth grade, I've been your biggest fan ... on your journey ... and that became my journey. Amber, your passion for life has always inspired me, and I'm better because of your friendship, but I've always felt like I was going along for the ride... I'm not complaining." Amber burst into tears. "Are you saying that our friendship has been fake?!" Wendy is quick to console her, "I'm not saying that at all. Your friendship ... we're sisters and you mean the world to me. I don't know how I would have made it through these years without you."

"So, stop this nonsense and pick up that phone and call Duke back. Now!" Amber demands. But, Wendy has made up her mind, "This is where I belong... for the first time in my life, I feel like I'm ... I'm ... not afraid of being on the inside... making a difference... and I have passion for it... for people... and I can't believe that I'm saying that... but I do. I care. And I want to continue with this passion..." Just as Wendy is beginning to feel relieved from the burden of having to break this news to her friend, Amber begins to sob uncontrollably.

She begins to gather her belongings as she yells at Wendy, "Why do I feel like you're breaking up with me? Well, you can abandon our dreams if you want to... but me... I'm going to Duke... I'm going to become that lawyer... I'm going to stick to the plan! And don't worry about the graduation party... I mean, what's the point?" Wendy says, "Amber, wait; calm down... I thought..." Amber reaches the door and walks out as Wendy finishes her statement, "... you of all people would understand..."

Wendy notices her mom, and just stares at her—speechless. Martha Lee says, "You okay?" "Yeah, Mom ... Ummm... how much of that conversation did you hear?" Martha Lee responds, matter-of-fact like, "Enough to know that... apparently, you're not going to Duke?" Wendy begins to whine, "Mom, can we talk about it later? I have some friends coming over in an hour...and the boys' father will be dropping them home soon as well."

Martha Lee inquires, "Friends?" "Chrissy and Brandon," Wendy explains, "We have some details to work out for the yearbook, and we want to plan a memorial service for all the young people who have lost their lives in this past year... including Mae..." Martha says, "Wendy, I don't know how I feel about you not going to Duke, but I'm proud of you... so very proud of you. We'll talk later." Martha Lee begins to move towards the kitchen to put her groceries away as Wendy follows close behind her.

Wendy hesitantly inquires of Martha Lee, "Mom, where's my Dad? I mean, who is he? What's the story? I... just want to know..." Martha freezes in her steps as Wendy very gently asks, "Can we talk, Mom?" Martha Lee is obviously startled. In all of the seventeen years of her daughter's life, not one time did this topic come up from either side. She looks at her daughter and says, "I thought you have friends coming over?" Wendy doesn't respond. Martha proceeds to put her bags down on the counter, and thoughtfully leads her daughter to the living room. There, they take a seat next to one other on the couch. Once settled, Martha Lee takes a deep breath, and then speaks. "Okay, I don't know if I'm ready for this. All these years and you've never asked. Why now?"

Wendy quickly responds, "It has to do with identity, I guess... Knowing who and where I've come from is going to help me better understand myself. What happened to him? Do I have relatives, cousins, uncles?" Embarrassed, Martha stutters, "I, well... I don't know..." "Okay. Well, what is his name? Am I like him?" Martha Lee answers again, "I don't know..." There is an awkward silence while Wendy tries to understand the, "I don't' know" part. "What do you mean, you don't know? Like ... you really don't know who my father is?"

There is a nervous tension that begins to overwhelm Martha Lee. She responds to it by blurting out her words, "I ran away from home... I was just running... away from everything! After my mother, your grandma died... I just didn't know. Lord, what am I trying to say? She had been dying for some time... cancer—and I felt like everything around me was dying. You know, cancer has a way of changing your world. My world was dying... then, you came along." Martha Lee acts as if she's finished with her explanation.

When Wendy gets it that her mother is trying to be done with the conversation, she objects, saying, "Mom, come on. What happened after cancer, and in between you running away and me coming along?" Martha Lee looks at her daughter and puts a warm smile on her face. She then makes the decision to enter into a real conversation with her daughter about her father.

"You brought life to my world... the child in my womb gave me the courage to face life again... you became my 'why'... Your existence and the hope of your future resurrected my world." She looks at her daughter and braces herself to reveal something she's never spoken out loud. "Rape... that's what happened." There is a noticeable reaction from Wendy. When Wendy pulls herself together, Martha Lee continues telling her story.

"You're not going to understand this right away, but your father wasn't a bad man. He was a stranger I encountered in the night as I walked home from the late shift. And I used to think he was a very evil person ... but how can an evil tree bring forth good fruit?" She looks into her daughter's eyes and talks directly to her. "You're this amazing creature. Pure, full of life and good. Whatever happened to your father changed him and he chose an evil path."

Her eyes remain fixed on her daughter as she pensively searches out Wendy's emotions. Satisfied with her findings, she continues. "As far as I know about him is that horrifying night. On that night, I felt my life was going to be over, but I was dead inside already. Afterwards, he said 'I'm sorry.' Then, he just left me in the park."

Somehow, I made it home, and I remember asking God why He let me live... and why didn't He just let me die already." A few months later, I knew that I was pregnant with you... and then, I knew why God let me live. I found the desire to live again because of the life in my womb. When you were born, I learned how to forgive..." "Wow, wow... I'm ... I don't know," says Wendy, "... Mom, I'm sorry."

Raising her voice to correct Wendy, Martha Lee cuts her off, "Don't be sorry. Never feel sorry for me for having you! Just do me this one favor..." When she feels she has her daughter's full attention, she speaks again. "Whenever you get to wondering about where you're from, remember this—I don't believe in coincidences... God knew what He was doing when he knit you together in my womb. And the seed He used? Well, that's His business. You just live your life in freedom to be you... and know whatever good is in you... it could've been from him or me. Wendy, know that your real identity is from God as He reveals Himself to you, in you and through you..."

Wendy is speechless and emotionless. They take a long moment to process the last few moments, after which, Wendy suddenly blurts out with confidence and resolve in her voice and attitude, "I'm not going to Duke. It makes more sense to me now. Mom, I know this sounds crazy and like I'm going off of my emotions, but until now, I used to think that it was because I don't know my father that I couldn't trust myself. Like I was waiting for some affirmation to feel validated, that I'm okay—or before people could like me—or that I had anything to give or say..." Wendy stops talking for a moment to gather her thoughts.

In that moment, a voice is heard from behind them, "Oh, hey y'all." Startled, both Wendy and Martha Lee jumped to their feet. Gurley has just popped up from behind the couch where she's been on the floor sleeping in a drunken stupor. Annoyed and attempting to calm her pounding heart, Martha Lee berates her sister. "Gurley! Girl, what are you doing? Where did you come from?" Have you been back behind the couch all along?!" Ignoring her sister's inquiry and reeking of alcohol, she asks, "Is dinner ready? I'm hungry..."

Just then, the doorbell rings, and as Wendy starts for the door, she complains, "Auntie! Can you please excuse yourself? Mamma, can you tell her, please?!" Wendy answers the door. Chrissy, Brandon, and Wander walk into the house. Wendy greets them and leads them to the living room as Martha Lee, as discreetly as possible, takes Gurley by the hand, leading her out of the living room and down the hall towards her bedroom.

Once they get settled, Wendy says, "Wander..." But she quickly cuts her off, correcting Wendy. "Oh, it's Deborah. I answer to Deborah now... and I hope you don't mind. Chrissy and Brandon said that it would be okay if I tagged along tonight." With a big smile on her face, Wendy says, "Yeah, you're fine, Deborah..." She lets her smile linger for a moment to reassure her. Then, she turns her attention to the group. "Well, let's get started if we are going to this revival tonight. We have the next two hours to put the final touches on the yearbook and plan the memorial. Brandon, you have your hard drive?"

Brandon exuberantly responds, "Yep, and I knocked an hour off our work for tonight. It's already done. Check out my presentation." Brandon begins to connect his USB drive to his computer. Meanwhile,

Chrissy clears her throat and says, "Umm, I have something to say." Brandon quickly responds, "Look, I'm not trying to take over. We can change anything that you're not happy with..."

"No, not that. Brandon, you're fine," says Chrissy. "I just wanna say thanks. Up until when I started working with you both, I had been pretty lonely. This is probably our last meeting as a team, and I just want to say, I'm going to miss you guys. You know, I didn't want to work at first, but this past year has been the best time of my life. Going on these photo shoots and writing these essays... I didn't know I could write like this... I've decided I'm going to study journalism at State University... I love the rush..."

As he continues working on his presentation setup, Brandon says, "I mean, who wouldn't want to do this for the rest of their lives... lights... camera... action?!" They all look at Wendy. She shrugs her shoulders before saying, "Hey, well... I wouldn't call it journalism for me... but I did accept that internship offer from Pastor Wynn. So, that means I'll be around. In fact, I've decided to go to State University too."

Brandon continues, "... and by the way, I'm going to State University... however, I've planned to go to

State since I came out of my mother's womb. You know, it's ranked among the top ten leading colleges in the nation... especially for the arts..." At this, they all look at Deborah. There is an awkward pause on her behalf. Then, she finally gets that they are waiting for her to share her future plans with them. "Oh, yeah, ..." she says. "Well, I'm just going to work on being Deborah for a while..." They all chuckle and begin to dive into their work for the evening.

# Chapter Ten

## But God!

A few weeks have passed, and it's one of those rare occasions when Martha Lee finds herself home alone, except for Pop-Pop who's napping in his room. The house is pleasantly quiet, but the mood is a bit somber. She's just arrived home from the community-wide memorial service honoring the young people who have lost their lives in the past year. Wendy and most of the yearbook committee planned the event as part of the high school's year-end events.

Martha Lee slipped out ahead of the benediction to get home in time to resolve a personal matter in privacy, and afterwards, make preparations for the small crowd of people from the memorial services expected to gather at her home in an hour or so. She emerges from her bedroom and moves swiftly to the kitchen still wearing her well-fitted black skirt suit, but she's changed into a classy pair of black fluffy house slippers.

The doorbell rings and startles Martha Lee, even though she's expecting it to do so.

She takes a moment to regulate her breathing. After which, she smooths out the imaginary wrinkles from her skirt as she makes her way to the door. In walks Eugene Jean. "Afternoon, Ms. Martha," he says as he nervously snatches his hat from his head and begins to make his way as far away from the door as possible. "Thank you for having me," he continues. "I see you're coming to your senses so that we can work through this thing together."

Ignoring this last statement, Martha Lee speaks with a stern but polite voice. "Thanks for coming, Eugene. Please have a seat... I do want to talk to you. After all, I think it's fair to give us some kinda chance for closure for the both of us..." "Absolutely, I'm happy that..." Eugene stops mid-stride on his way to the couch. "Wait, what did you just say?! Closure? You do mean in the sense that we can get an understanding about my ... wife... soon to be ex-wife, so that we—the both of us—can move on from here? Correct?!" He stands perfectly still, waiting on Martha Lee's confirmation.

"Weeellll, this is what I want to talk to you about." She motions him to the couch where she has just taken a seat, and then continues talking as he makes his way to his seat. "I've been thinking and... now, I've given this a lot of thought... so I don't want you to think I'm taking this lightly—you and me—but..." There is an awkward moment of silence as Eugene takes his seat.

The moment proves too long for Eugene, so he breaks the silence. "But... but what, Ms. Martha? What?!... Lord, this doesn't sound so good... you need to go on and say what you need to say! Now, I can admit it; I have been very careless. I should've told you the truth from the very beginning or been willing to lose that old house in order to gain such a beautiful, good woman. You, Ms. Martha Lee, you're what I choose... I consider you more valuable than rubies and gold... and..." He's sounding a bit too rehearsed for Martha Lee. She puts her hands up to signal him to stop talking.

"Ah, Eugene, I think you should let me speak..." She takes a moment to change her composure and then begins her own semi-rehearsed speech. "I, ... for these last years.... I." She sighs at not being able to get the words out like she'd rehearsed, so she just settles on being herself and speaking from her heart. She continues, and this time, she actually looks and sounds more relaxed. "It's not you, Eugene. I believe you when you say you haven't lived as husband and wife all these years. My position is this... it's between you and your estranged wife regarding what you do with your marriage. You say you're dissolving it on account of me and you... after all these years."

She takes a moment to clear her throat, "Regrettably, I've settled for someone's second thought after all these years, and I never knew. Well, that speaks loud! Wouldn't you say?! I know It speaks to me. It speaks to me on what I've been missing... all these years. A sense of who I am, what I want, and most importantly, where and when I went wrong. Eugene, I realized, after all these years that I need to figure things out. Now, figuring things out is my responsibility." She stops for a moment to let him take in what she's just said to him.

With raised eyebrows, she asks, "Didn't you think I ever wondered why I never got an invite to your house?" She bows her head and begins to shake it in despair, "We weren't a normal couple... I just—and you did too... we settled. Not with each other, but we just kinda accepted what came to us, rather than pursue with purpose. That's why your secret lasted all these years... we settled."

She takes another deep breath, slowly exhales, and then continues. "For this reason, I need for you to say goodbye. Let me go. I need to figure out some things, and I need to do that alone. I need room enough to change my mind if I need to. And not just about us, but about my life, my career..." She rises to her feet, expecting him to do the same. He finally does, but begins to object to her finality. "Now, Ms. Martha, we've got to... I have something to say... I need to..." But Martha Lee begins to walk him towards the door.

"Eugene," she says with a lot of resolve, "I've loved you... it may have been an inadequate love... I don't know. I need to... I need you to respect my wishes. Now, go deal with your life, as I will mine. Goodbye." Finally convinced, Eugene drops his head and says his goodbyes. "Martha Lee... take care of yourself. You take care of yourself, you hear?" Martha Lee closes the door and takes a moment to breathe as Gurley appears from the bedroom area.

She's dressed sloppily, still in her sleep attire and, by all appearances, she could be drunk. She makes a staggering beeline to the fridge. Noticing Martha Lee standing at the door, she casually speaks to her, "Oh hey, Mamma. What are you doing?" Martha Lee dryly answers her, "I'm in the middle of cleaning house! I didn't know you were here. I peeked in your room and didn't see you or the boys. Are they...?" Gurley cuts her off with a hoarse laugh, "Oh yeah, I just woke up. Girl, I had fallen asleep in the closet. The boys, they are with their dad for some quality time..." She begins to laugh again. Martha Lee glares at her sister as if she's wondering if Gurley has lost her mind. As her blood runs hot through her veins, she raises her voice enough to emphasize her seriousness. "Gurley, this is the absolute last day you will be drunk in my house!" Gurley nonchalantly answers her sister, "What?! I'm not drunk... just a little hung over... any ginger ale?" She begins to rummage through the refrigerator.

Martha Lee continues with the same tone as she lays out the new rules with authority. "This is the last month you will be jobless in my house... as of now, you're on notice..." Gurley objects, "But Mamma, I just..." Martha cuts her off, "Hush... and this is the last time you will call me mamma... I'm your sister and you're going to start acting like it." Before Gurley can respond, the doorbell rings. As Martha Lee crosses to answer the door, she continues to give orders to Gurley. "Now, go get presentable so we can support Vera and the kids as a family!"

The finality in Martha Lee's voice signals Gurley to submit to her sister's orders. She immediately stops what she's doing and begins to make her way to her bedroom as Martha gathers her composure. As she opens the door, Vera, April and Junie stand, dressed in black and huddled together as if posing for a family portrait. Martha invites them in and shows them to the sitting room as Gurley disappears down the hallway.

"I'm really sorry for this bother, Ms. Martha," says Vera, "but I had nowhere else to go to make this easier for my kids..." Martha Lee says, "Nonsense, Vera. We are honored to be a support to you and the kids." Vera continues as if she didn't hear Martha's encouragement. "I don't know how we're going to be okay after this, but that's what they keep telling me, so that's what I keep telling my kids."

As Vera finishes her statement and begins to tend to the children, Wendy, Chrissy, Brandon and Deborah (previously know as Wander), arrive from the memorial services. They begin to gather in the kitchen as Martha Lee continues her conversation with Vera. "Honestly, Vera, it's going to be okay. Handing these babies over to the system is just temporary. You'll be working and have these babies back before you know it. Do you know how I know? Because you've done everything right since the judge's ruling. You've begun taking parenting classes, financial classes; you've found a good church home... you have a support system..."

People from the memorial service begin to fill the house. Among them are Principal McClain, Mrs. Stance and Savannah. The ladies promptly make their way to the kitchen to relieve themselves of the food trays each of them are carrying. After placing her tray in the small space she found on the kitchen counter, Principal McClain flashes a big grin and begins to speak to the group. "Wendy, Brandon, Chrissy—job well done! Barbara, this year's yearbook has really proven to be the best one yet! So raw and real!"

"Yes," exclaims Barbara. "I say the same. Chrissy, that article you wrote for the yearbook on Charles T. Turner Technical High School's commitment to the well-being and safety of the kids in this community made the Tribune newspaper. Well done. You've turned into quite the journalist. And yes, Brandon, the newspaper is using some of your most compelling photos..." Branden beams with joy and a huge smile begins to appear on his face as the reality of what was told him starts to set in.

"Honestly, Brandon," says Principal McClain. "You can start a movement for social change with your eye for photography." She turns to Wendy and speaks directly to her. "I have watched you blossom over these last few months... You have the stuff that leaders who really make a difference in our world have... After you graduate, I hope that whatever you decide to do, you will do it with ownership. Go out there and continue to TAKE A STAND FOR CHANGE..." She talks to the four of them, "Own your identity and pursue your purposes with passion and boldness..."

At this, Barbara cuts in reciting the school's motto, "Making today's leaders." She chuckles, "Well, we have certainly kept the school's vision statement...in a big way, wouldn't you say?!... How about that memorial service?" "It was genius for the yearbook committee to host it," says Principal McClain. Savannah chimes in, "Yes, the service sent a clear message—the need for safety for our kids in the community."

Principal McClain beams with pleasure, "Standing room only... Even the mayor and police chief attended... oh, and we sold out of the yearbooks... we have to reorder so that the seniors can get their copies..." Savannah continues, "That segment you did on Mae and her family's crisis was so tastefully done too." She turns toward Vera, and with a pleasant smile, greets her from across the room. "Hello again, Vera. Our condolences to you. We know it's a tough time for you, but we are here for you."

Wendy waves to Vera and greets her, "Oh, hello Ms. Vera. What did you think of our tribute to Mae?" Vera responds with both sadness and gratuity in her voice, "Today? It was good... and the people heard me and my kids' story. Tomorrow will come and people will soon forget, but I'm still living and I guess I have to keep living..." Tears well up in her eyes. The toddler she's holding is a bit restless, but Junie, who is unusually quiet, takes the toddler out of his mother's arms and begins to whisper in her ear to quiet her.

All eyes are on Vera. There is a somber quietness for a moment while Vera gathers her thoughts to speak. "I wanted to die! But, I just didn't know what to do with my babies... I even thought about how to do it. Make it look like an accident so they wouldn't have a bad opinion about me for leaving my kids." She stops for a moment, then continues with tears streaming down her cheeks. "Mae beat me to it." She looks around at the crowd and, feeling the need to defend her words, she continues, "I'm a good mother. Well, at least, the best I knew how... been on my own since I was 14-years old. Nobody helped me. I've been in a failed life even before I was born, it seems. Homeless, penniless, helpless... I come from foster care, you know. Now, they're putting my kids there."

Her voice cracks as she tries hard to keep herself together, "I was just trying to do my best—you know—to get by. I never took drugs, not a taste of alcohol, not even a cigarette. God, have I been cursed with this life? What did I do? Now, they tell me Mae is dead and gone, never coming back ..." She begins to wipe her tears and nose on the cuff of her sleeve as if to demonstrate her determination to suck up the pain of saying goodbye. "Well, goodbye, Mae! I tried to tell you life is not fair and death can sneak up on you…, but you wouldn't listen... now you dead... but, you the lucky one ..."

Junie, who has been listening while holding his little sister, April, and trying to process what his mother is conveying, anxiously cries, "But Mommy, what about us? We love you... I can help... you still have me and April. I can be a good help..." It's a difficult moment for everyone, but especially for Vera with her son. She softly responds with her hand held up to reject his comfort, "Get away boy... you can't help what's inevitable."

Martha Lee rushes to the boy's side and takes his baby sister out of his arms. She then gives them both the most comforting hug she knows how to give. "There, there. It's going to be okay. Hold on, son. God will take care of this..." Junie, not able to hold back his tears, begins to sob as he asks a heart-wrenching question, "But, why is God letting this happen? Is He mad at me? Is He mad at my mommy?" At this, Savannah falls to one knee in order to look Junie in his eyes as she encourages him.

She says, "Now, you hear me really good, son. This right here is a hard time for your family, but God is not letting this happen to you in order to crush you. Something good will come of this. Even when we don't feel it, God is always working for our good... take this as truth from me, son. Even when the dimmest times come, God will shine a light in the darkness... He's a way maker, miracle worker..." Almost on cue, Principal McClain begins to sing the song, "... light in the darkness, that is who you are..."

As she continues to sing, Amber arrives and immediately goes to hug Wendy. They embrace as they join the small crowd who's now singing along with Principal McClain. During the singing, Wendy has noticed the many notifications that have been popping up on her phone. Whatever she's reading has made her eyes grow three sizes bigger and her mouth drop to the floor, it would seem. She begins to hush the singers with hand motions as her voice booms over them.

"Ooooooh, snap! My gosh!" She turns the phone screen around and first shows Amber what she's reading, and then Brandon, Chrissy, and finally Deborah. They all grow pale one after another as they get a glimpse of Wendy's phone message. Then, she turns toward the crowd of people to let them in on the news. "You remember the go-fund me account we started for Ms. Vera and her family? Well apparently, the tribute to Mae brought attention to it." She quickly goes to her mom and shows her the proof, and then to a few others in the crowd. Finally, she makes her way over to Ms. Vera. But, before she shows it to her, Wendy continues, "So far, of the five-thousand-dollar goal we wanted to raise for you, we've raised $88,000! No kidding! Look, Ms. Vera..."

Vera quickly grabs the phone and begins to read as everyone erupts with celebration! As she reads, she begins to weep until her body begins to shudder with joy. She then turns to her children, Junie and April, to embrace them. Principal McClain begins to sing the song *Way Maker* again as the small crowd gathers around the family to congratulate Vera and her children and sing along.

Afterwards, Pop-Pop staggers up the hallway and into the midst of the crowd. Something about how he's standing commands the people's attention. Then, he says, "Romans 8:28, 'And we know that all things work together for good to them that love God, to them who are the called according to His purpose.'" In the stark quietness, he staggers back down the hallway, and before disappearing into his bedroom, he says, "God said that."

And all the people said, "Amen" and "Hallelujah!"

The End!